THE POINT

Titles By Colleen Charles

Dangerous Pasts:

Closing The Gap
Song Of The Keys
Stacking The Deck

Minnesota Caribou:

Benched
Played
Checked

Rochester Riot:

The Slot
The Crease
The Point

Reel Love:

Bait
Hook
Line
Sinker

The Caldwell Brothers:

Hard Gamble
Tightwad
Kickback
Pony Up
All In
Raincheck
On The House

Dangerous Futures:

Stone Cold Love

Pagan Passion:

Solstice Song

Taboo Tales:

Chopped
Roped
Educated

Romance Singles:

Hot Cakes

Hot Water

Hot Pursuit

Downfall

Chaos & Class

Crabbypants

Mansplainer

Gunslinger

THE POINT

A Rochester Riot Hockey Romance

Book Three – Ryder & Hannah

Colleen Charles

The Point Copyright © 2020
by Colleen Charles

Printed in the United States of America
First Printing, 2020

ISBN: 9798690838539

Second Wind Publishing

www.ColleenCharles.com

FOREWORD

Subscribe to my Newsletter online and receive email notices about new book releases, sales, and special promotions.

New subscribers receive an EXCLUSIVE FREE NOVEL as a special gift.

www.colleencharles.com/free

CHAPTER ONE

Hannah

"You look gorgeous," I said, fluffing her skirt.

"You think so?" Sophia Robertson asked with a sigh. I didn't think I'd ever seen my sister this beautiful, this happy. Hearing her words tugged at something deep inside, as did the way the soft swish of satin caressed Sophia's skin, skimming every curve of her body. A stab of jealousy started in my spine and traveled outward to cause some annoying tingles in my limbs.

Bitten by the green-eyed monster again.

It seemed I could never live up to my sisters. Not Eloise and her intelligent yet sexy capabilities or Sophia and her romantic softness. With a weary sigh, I glanced down at my fit and trim body. I'd never have what Eloise and Sophia had without a visit to the plastic surgeon, and who wanted to carve themselves up in the name of beauty? I could almost hear my mother's admonishments blistering my ears even though she'd already left her daughters alone in the bedroom.

"I've always thought so," Eloise said, interrupting my slow trek on the pity train as she spun Sophia around. "Wedding or no wedding, Phil Pomeroy is getting the most beautiful girl in the world. Inside and out." El's arms went around Sophia's neck, enveloping her in sisterly love. "I love the dress."

"Me too," Sophia gushed. "I can't believe it's tomorrow. I've waited so many years for this, El. You can't even imagine..."

"Oh, but I can imagine. You forget that I've been exactly where you are, little sister. Thinking I might never get the love I deserve. But I've had my happily ever after and now you're getting yours. I wish you nothing but happiness, Soph. You deserve it."

I approached Eloise and draped my body over both of them. "Group hug, Robertsons! I'm in the room, too. Or have you already forgotten your poor, lonely, pathetic single sister? Just because I don't have some hot guy to hold my hand doesn't mean I'm not part of the family."

Sophia and Eloise included me in their tear-jerker moment, and we stayed that way in a ring of arms and emotion until Eloise finally broke away to dab at her eyes. Sophia extended an arm to me. "Oh, come here, Hanna-bee. We wouldn't let you miss out on a thing. We love you more than anything. The Three Robertson Girls until the end!"

I returned the smile and leaned in to give Eloise a kiss on her cheek, my long auburn waves falling into my sister's face as I did so. Eloise blew the tresses off her nose with a hiss of breath, causing my hair to fly so far backward it flounced through the air. We laughed and bumped fists.

"You'd better not ever forget about me," I said, tucking the flyaway locks behind my ears. "You've both left me behind in the romance department, eating your dust. I have to live vicariously through your love lives."

And even my sisters didn't know how desolate it really was. I crawled across a barren, arid desert while my sisters traipsed through an English garden complete with floral circlets and tambourines, colorful ribbons in their wake.

After our embrace – an unbreakable ring of love that felt stronger than any wedding band – Eloise clucked her tongue and stared at me with that big sister look.

"You'll find the right man someday, Hannah," Sophia said. "Just you wait and see. You're only twenty-three, for heaven's sake. Plenty of time. And you've got grad school ahead of you. Tons of smart, talented guys on campus, you lucky thing. Wish I could do college all over again. I'd do it right this time."

I rolled my eyes. "What would you do over?"

Sophia grinned. "Can you believe I never went to a toga party, and I never had a one-night stand? Now, I'm afraid that ship has sailed. Only one man for me for the rest of my life. You should kick it hard while you're young and you still can. Besides, since you're the youngest, Mom stays off your case. Mostly."

"Are you kidding, Soph?" I said with a laugh, breaking free from my sisters. "She's laser focused on me now that both of you are honest women. She wants to dig her nose into all of my business, and she can track mischief like a bloodhound on an escapee's scent. After the wedding, she'll be coming at me full force. Just because you've found your destiny with ol' Philbert, doesn't mean she'll completely let you off the hook."

Eloise laughed and I turned toward her. "And you... you've snagged the hottest hockey hunk of all time. That Beantown Bard didn't take long to lock shit down."

Eloise just beamed, her smile brighter than the sun. "Lock shit down? For a soon to be grad student, you sound more like a middle schooler," she said. "But Cole and I married at exactly the right time. We both just knew we didn't want to wait. Since our wedding, there hasn't been time for much else besides renovating the restaurant and running the marketing campaign. Cole's already in pre-season practice, so I'm pretty much carrying the puck, so to speak. But I admit that I really love my new gig as wife and business owner. Never a dull moment."

"That's not all you're carrying," Sophia said with a knowing smile, carefully removing her wedding dress and hanging it in its place of honor in the closet until the next day. "And I, for one, can't wait to meet the new addition."

El glanced down and stroked a palm over her rounded belly and shook her head. "My life is blessed. After everything I went through back in high school... let's just say I'm filled with gratitude for everything turning out in my favor."

My sigh blew my bangs skyward. "I think I'm going to drown in all this blessedness," I said while waving a hand across the room. "Girls just want to have fun, you know. Even I have heard the anthem of Cyndi Lauper."

"We'd never leave you behind, Hanna-bee. You know that," Sophia said. "You go out and have your fun, and we'll support you. We'll even try to divert mom's attention so you can do whatever it is you college girls are doing nowadays. Just don't visit that smarmy Ivy League school. I'm still shocked by that disgusting video of those frat boys there. Can you believe such an exclusive and admired institution could have something like that happen?"

Eloise scrunched up her nose and pouted. "I know. Vile. Absolutely despicable."

I looked from sister to sister, not knowing what the hell they were talking about. "Huh?"

"You didn't see it," Sophia spat. "They went marching across campus with signs that said, 'No means yes and yes means anal.' I can't believe you didn't hear about it."

I reared back, appalled. "Are you kidding me?"

Eloise finally found her voice. "I only wish we were kidding. Just make sure you fully vet your possible one-night stands before you indulge."

My stomach clenched. Why were college aged guys so immature? "I will. That's really scary. Like that time El dragged me into the woods to search for you, Soph. I could barely keep up. I hate being scared."

"You remember that?" Sophia asked, her brow creasing.

"You were only what, six?" El queried.

"Seven. And yes, I do. Scariest night of my life. But it sounds like the Yale guys are even more terrifying. Good thing no more undergrad. It's time to grow up. Good grief!"

A delicate frown passed over Sophia's face. "That night wasn't half as scary for you as it was for me. I was so confident I knew my way around. But I was so angry that I stomped off without thinking. At the time, I didn't want anyone to find me." She brightened and turned to Eloise. "I'm glad you didn't give up on me."

"Never," El said, shaking her head. "And Mom and Dad wouldn't either. In fact, they're waiting downstairs. C'mon. The wedding rehearsal is in two hours, we'd better get going. No family drama, okay? It's not good for baby Fiorino."

As Eloise and Sophia made their way to the main floor of the house, I hung back. Oddly enough, I did remember that night in the woods, or at least my dreamlike, childhood rendition of it. Mom and Sophia yelling at each other. Mom and Dad leaving, going out somewhere. Being the eldest, Eloise was in charge, as always, when we were alone. Next thing I knew, Eloise had me by the hand and was dragging me out the back gate, looking for Sophia. What had they argued about? My seven-year-old brain hadn't understood but knew it was something bad. Shaking off the memory, I focused on the present.

Making Sophia's day the best day of her life.

I truly wanted to be excited and happy for my sisters, but my own feelings kept rearing their ugly little heads. I'd lived in this same aging four-bedroom ranch in Columbus, Ohio my whole life, and though I loved my parents, I couldn't wait to get away from them and the stifling constraints of my childhood. Could a woman be repressed by too much love and care? Sometimes I thought so.

Fleeing the fam, however, was easier said than done. Then again, Eloise had done it with aplomb.

I frowned as my fingers touched the wrinkled and worn envelope in my jeans pocket. Carefully unfolding it, I viewed its contents for at least the tenth time, somehow hoping the words had changed since my last reading.

Tears blurred the words together, but I still knew they hadn't

Dear Miss Robertson, after a thorough review of your application, we regret to inform you that your admission to Franklin University is denied at this time. While your academic records show promise, our enrollment limit compels us to give preference to those applicants with the highest grade point average. We encourage you to re-apply for the winter admission.

I hadn't told my parents. They'd be too disappointed. I cringed at their expressions as I imagined having to break the news. Unlike my sisters, I was not a star student. Studying didn't come easily, and I'd finished undergrad with a solid, if unremarkable, B- average.

Worse, I had no idea or inclination which field I wanted to pursue for my master's, but I didn't want to stop and just get a safe but unremarkable job. I wanted to make a difference in the world, and follow my bliss, but I still wasn't sure what I wanted to be when I grew up. I seemed to just be flitting through life. My interests in school were scattered, never settling on any one thing, so I'd declared a general business major only after threats from my advisor.

Without much thought, I'd applied to the accounting program at Franklin University right in Columbus. Though I had to laugh at myself for choosing something so completely at odds with my distinctly un-mathematical personality, the rejection letter in my pocket was no laughing matter. While a career was expected of me, what I really wanted was what my sisters had managed to find in addition to stellar careers – a marriage to the love of their lives. And babies. Lots of babies.

Is that so wrong? So old-fashioned?

Allowing my eyes to flutter closed, I imagined walking down the aisle tomorrow instead of Sophia. What would my groom look like? Tall, dark-haired, his broad shoulders covered in an expensive Armani suit. He'd be wealthy of course; a classy corporate type, maybe a lawyer or a doctor. Nah. Not a doctor. And never a smarmy lawyer. An accountant? Yeah, that was it. With glasses. There'd be plenty of those if I ever made it into Franklin.

The winter admission period wouldn't open until January. What would I do until then? The thought of rattling around my parents' house in my same-old-same-old hometown for another six months or more made me want to run off into the woods just like Sophia had done.

"Hannah!"

My eyes snapped open at the sound of Eloise's voice. Next to our mother's, Eloise's was the voice I obeyed – the hand of command. My feet moved automatically to comply.

"Coming!" I yelled.

***

Sophia's wedding day unfolded like a dreamy fairytale. I felt hypnotized as I took my place next to Eloise and watched our middle sister proceed slowly toward us on our father's arm. He looked so handsome. As they drew near to the dais, Sophia's train with the little satin rosebuds stitched into it seemed a mile long, whispering gently against the carpet with each step forward. To my left, Phil Pomeroy waited with his groomsmen. He wasn't the most handsome thing on two legs, but in his tux and grinning from ear to ear, I had to admit he looked sharp. And deliriously happy.

You are so lucky, Soph.

A tiny sigh escaped. Was that how every man looked when he was about to be married? I hoped so, and wondered, *where oh where is the man who will have that look on his face when he gazes upon me*? My knees trembled a little as the ceremony went on, listening to the pastor's monotone recitation and various readings from a few of Sophia's friends. With the rush of activity before the event, we hadn't eaten much, and my stomach growled. As lovely as the wedding was, I couldn't wait for it to be over and get to the good part – the food and drinks. And dancing. Maybe I'd meet someone at the reception. Everyone always raved about weddings as a target rich environment where people were already in pair-up mode.

At last, the happy couple kissed and marched triumphantly out of the sanctuary to the strains of Mendelssohn played by the string quartet Sophia had insisted upon. My ears still rang from Sophia's fight with our overbearing mother in regard to the playlist for the ceremony.

"I'm starving," I whispered to Eloise as we assembled in the vestibule for the obligatory receiving line.

"I don't remember you being a big eater as a kid," Eloise chuckled. "A tad fussy, as I recall."

I bristled. "Fussy? I'm fussy about lots of things, but right now, I feel like I could eat a buffalo. A cow just wouldn't be enough."

"Careful what you wish for," came a voice from aside. Eloise's eyes widened as she glanced past my shoulder. I turned toward the sound.

Russ Pomeroy, Phil's younger brother, stood there, an awkward grin on his face. "Oh, Russ," I said, wishing it was someone, anyone, else. Something inappropriate and uncomfortable was going to follow. I just knew it. "It's you."

"Russ," Eloise acknowledged.

"If you wanted bison on the buffet, you should have called my store," he said, puffing his scrawny chest out with pride and fake bravado. Russ was part-owner of the local butcher shop, and as a result never seemed quite able to rid himself of the singular odor of the place. I sniffed and exhaled quickly to rid my nostrils of the lingering scent of dead animal. Didn't the guy ever try after-shave or cologne? Eau de red meat didn't do it for me.

"I'll remember that for the next wedding," Eloise said in an effort to smooth over the moment.

Russ's grin grew wider as he cleared his long blond bangs from his face with a shake of his head. He appeared to have talked his way out of the barber shop date Phil had set with his groomsmen in some kind of loser hair strike. His skater-boy locks looked as messy as ever, and I felt suddenly glad that food industry workers were required to wear hats.

He fixed a sly eye on me and shot a hungry look my way. Right at the exposed cleavage of my low neckline. Damn Sophia and these revealing get-ups she'd chosen. Of course, Princess Eloise, matron of honor, had demanded a different style. One that covered her swollen boobs and flowed right over her baby bump.

"Maybe that will be me and Hanna-bee here," Russ said, winking.

"Right," Eloise laughed. "Get in line, kiddo." She gestured to the line of guests forming to greet the wedding party, but her double meaning was not lost on him or me.

Wearing an enigmatic smile, Russ nodded and moved off to join the queue. "Oh my God," I groaned. "I can't believe he said that. How dare he *do* that? We hardly know each other."

"I can't believe he called you Hanna-bee. How does he even know that nickname?" She turned a pointed stare to me. "Have you guys been dating? How come I don't know about this?" she asked, her perfectly-tinted lips curling up on one side.

How dare she tease me about an asshat?

I rolled my eyes and adjusted my now sweaty grip on the stem of the bouquet I held. The toe of my dyed satin pump stomped double time into the worn carpet of the church. Russ Pomeroy gave me the creeps. "Are you insane? We are *not* dating! And you're *not* funny! I wouldn't be caught dead with that Tony Hawk wearing, *Game of Thrones* watching, *Minecraft* playing blob of male b.s. He obviously has some weird fantasy about us. Once his brain cells fire and collide, we'll have evidence of spontaneous combustion."

Eloise threw her hands up into the air as if she were warding off a violent attack, but the upward tugging of her lips gave her away. "I just hope his weird fantasy doesn't include you sprawled naked on his butcher board, splayed open to receive the hot beef injection," Eloise wisecracked, finally giving in to her mirth at my expense. "How long has this been going on? I mean his... crush?"

I snorted a non-laugh. "Ugh, feels like forever. Mostly since Sophia and Phil's little breakup last year. When they got back together, Russ seemed to tag along whenever Phil started to come around again. Then the mindless chitchat started, and whenever he sees me, he won't stop. I feel like one of those people with nosy neighbors who hide in their garage and don't even check their mail."

"Well, he's in the family now," Eloise said. "Like it or not.

Just hope Mom doesn't get wind of it, or she'll catapult him in your direction like one of those human cannonballs we used to see when the circus came to town."

"Yeah, he'd look great in a red spandex leotard with a giant "R" splayed across his scrawny chest."

Our discussion was cut short as the line of guests offering handshakes and congratulations reached us. I shuddered at the thought of being related to Russ Pomeroy. Would that make him back off or just encourage him to pursue me more? I took the opportunity to warm my arms with my palms until I was occupied with Sophia's guests. I wished I'd applied to a faraway college, like El had. But it was too late to have a hope of getting in anywhere now, at least until the next admission period. The idea of being stuck in Columbus for another half year became more oppressing by the minute, suffocating me. I had to get out somehow.

Hanna-bee. I frowned at the name – one that had stuck after I'd dressed up as a bumblebee for Halloween one year in a padded yellow suit with black stripes. I'd always liked all things nature and allowed Eloise and Sophie all the princess fantasies, preferring to stand out from the crowd. How old had I been? Nine or ten? Later, my big sisters took to calling me 'Wanna-bee,' especially when I insisted on tagging along with them when I wasn't wanted. They teased that I always 'wanted' something, which was usually true. But deep down, what I wanted most was to be like them – all grown up and pretty and smart.

And in love.

Plenty of people told me I was pretty. I liked yellow, but I disliked the infantile reference that seemed to keep me perpetually tied to my childhood.

Time for Hanna-bee to leave the hive. Time to buzz away.

CHAPTER TWO

Ryder

The ice reflected an ethereal glow in the absence of overhead lights. As I sat on the cold plastic stadium seat, I breathed deeply of the chilled air inside Rochester Arena. The darkness enveloped me like a warm blanket despite the temperature. I inhaled, loving the smell of the rink. It made me feel so alive. Like I finally belonged somewhere.

The exit and emergency lights cast streaks of red and blue across the smooth, translucent surface that spread a hundred feet in either direction from my position at center ice. I imagined myself on the other side of the boards, blades carving and legs striding, waiting for that sweet pass onto the tape of my stick. Carrying. Shooting.

Scoring.

Arcing behind the net with my arms raised in victory.

I'd been there. Done that. Many times over throughout my life.

But never *here*, on the most hallowed ground of all. An NHL rink.

I heard a faint noise from the direction of the press box and roused myself from my daydream. Only the click of an automated switch of some arena control or other, but enough to make me jump to my feet.

How stupid would I look, if the lights suddenly snapped on and one of the team or its staff caught me in here alone, communing with the rink spirits and my own elusive dreams? I might as well have been on my knees at a church altar, praying to the hockey gods. Fat lot of good prayer would do me at this point. I felt like a demon with sixes etched into the back of my neck. I was just as much a pariah in the hockey community as Damien had been to the Catholic Church. A nothing. A nobody.

Even being a fucking has-been would be better than being a never-was.

I made my way silently through the aisle and down the steps that led to the arena concourse. No one around at this time of day, with the official start of the hockey season still a few weeks away. The Rochester Riot would start another season soon, and then this frozen cathedral would come alive with screaming, rowdy worshipers once more, laying down beer, popcorn, and shreds of their soul to their men on the ice.

Once more, they'd sway, chant, and dance, hoping to incite a victory, but all their antics did for me was to taunt and agonize – remind me of the life that could have been. How I'd been passed over by the big leagues and my youthful hockey dreams crushed to something resembling the pile of Zamboni leavings dumped outside a community rink, telling me in no uncertain terms that the NHL career I coveted would never be mine.

I stomped a loafered toe into the floor, wishing I could create a divot and send debris flying along with my regret. Sure, I could have gone to Europe and played with a national team. There were other ways to make a living as a hockey player, I knew that. But my degree in marketing also provided opportunities to stay close to the game and make a nice living.

My job as a sales manager with the Rochester Riot still made me an employee of the NHL and therefore bestowed an implied pedigree. The money wasn't bad either; no seven-figure payroll like my old frenemy Cole Fiorino, but enough to buy me plenty of chicks, Joseph Abboud suits, and my beloved Lexus RC

Coupe that I drove to work every day and around town every night, finding sweet pussy to keep my winter nights a little warmer.

But none of that shit could hold a candle to the allure of being an actual player on the team. After making the junior all-stars along with many of the friends I'd grown up playing hockey with, and a notable three-year performance with my college team, I'd thought there was no way the scouts and the system could pass me by.

I'd thought wrong.

Dead. Ass. Wrong.

The NHL had never come knocking. Snubbed in my first draft-eligible year, I'd held my disappointment inside as best I could, but those around me knew better. I sulked. I moped. I beat the shit out of the bags at the boxing gym. I banged so many puck bunnies with sunflower bangs, I half expected to shoot seeds out my ass. I spent my savings traveling all over the damn country to attend club training camps as a walk-on, but with no success. Though others tried to sympathize, but no one could ever know the depths of my despair or my feelings of betrayal.

Because hockey – the thing I loved above all else – had stabbed me in the back.

Ryder Martin. Yeah, who the fuck am I? I doubt my own father even knows.

Shaking off my misty, time-tunneled thoughts, I glanced around the steel and concrete cavern of Rochester Arena. This was my life now. On the periphery perhaps, but still part of the dynasty. Better just accept it for what it was and move the hell on with whatever the future held.

I should feel lucky, and I did – most of the time. With my thirties beckoning, I wasn't getting any younger, and my options were narrowing. The pussy-train I'd enjoyed a few years ago no longer made such frequent whistle-stops at my station, either. As a 'suit' I didn't capture the interest of the hockey-wife hopefuls, so I'd set my sights on a loftier target. That curvaceous, feisty epitome of female perfection, Eloise Robertson, the Riot's former Community Relations Director.

Emphasis on former. After one disastrous dinner date, during which the fetching but frosty Eloise had sliced off my balls in a philosophical debate over labor unions, she'd fallen directly into the arms of the fabled Riot forward Cole Fiorino. Talk about emasculation? That woman made taking a man down a peg look like Romper Room.

They'd invited me to the wedding, but I'd graciously declined. I'd conceded enough failures without watching the entire documentary unfold before my eyes in living color. Knowing the woman I'd imagined as the mother of my children sucked Fiorino's huge cock night after night was soul crushing enough.

He had every motherfucking thing I wanted and then some.

As I walked the curved halls of the arena, I spotted a familiar face. Shane McTaggart, the newly appointed coach of the Rochester Riot, stepped into the corridor from one of the skybox entrances.

"Shane," I called as I strode toward the gruff coach, a rare grin tugging my lips.

Shane's impeccably groomed red-haired head with graying temples swiveled in his direction. "As I live and breathe," Shane chuckled. "If it isn't Ryder Martin. I heard you were working out here in Minne-land." Shane McTaggart extended a broad hand to me.

"Oh yeah, me and Paul Bunyan go way back," I answered, receiving the hearty handshake. "Just don't say I resemble

Babe the Blue Ox."

"So you hung up the blades in exchange for a suit, eh?" McTaggart continued, shaking his head. "Who'd have figured? Thought you'd prefer shredding the ice instead of shredding sensitive corporate documents."

I smiled, trying to conceal my well-worn but ever-present chagrin over my career outcome. My pearly whites ground against each other as I did so. "Luckily, Eloise Fiorino used to run this joint, and she kept us all on the straight and narrow. No shredding of paper necessary. As for me, well... choices, my friend and not preferences. Low risk, high reward."

"Totally understand," Shane agreed, "Hard to melt the ice from your veins, though, isn't it?"

"Hey, I still play," I said in mock defense, spreading my arms wide. "You're looking at a star beer-leaguer. Don't knock it until you try it. There's minimal travel, and booze and floozies at the end." I'd played for McTaggart once upon a time and was pleased to learn of his appointment to the Riot's bench. Shane knew everything there was to know about my hockey skills. Shane was one hell of a coach and a damn good human being.

"Yeah?" Shane rubbed a hand across his stubbled chin as he looked me up and down. "This may be jumping the gun," he said, leaning in a bit. "But if you think you've still got what it takes, the league is about to announce a crazy promo. They're holding open tryouts in September, awarding a one-year contract on each team for a newcomer, to be put on waivers if the team doesn't pick them up." He cocked his head. "Publicity stunt for sure. You know how it goes when it comes to that money hungry pain in our ass, Sheehan Murphy. Old coot thought up the scheme all by his little lonesome, and I'll be damned if he won't make millions off it. But you still might want to think about it. Get yourself in shape, old-timer." Shane swatted me in my suited midsection. "You'd have a good chance at it."

I jerked on reflex, but even more in surprise. *Open tryouts*? "Get the fuck out," I said, unbelieving. "Why would Sheehan do that? I can't imagine any amount of money means that much to Sheehan and the other owners that they'd have a bunch of rejects skating around their billion-dollar facilities, stinking them up."

McTaggart shrugged. "Like I said. Publicity stunt. Get the fans fired-up for a hometown hero. Local boy does good and all that. Sells more tickets. And the Riot could definitely use some positive publicity after the Bernie Griffiths incident."

I sobered at the mention of Griffiths. Found murdered in the arena parking garage a year earlier, the Riot's short-term COO and friend of owner Sheehan Murphy had cast an undeniable shadow over last season. They'd fallen short of hockey's Holy Grail once more and could certainly use a distraction this year like the one Shane described. Maybe Murphy was a fucking genius after all.

"True," I said, letting the idea sink in. In the realm of second chances, this was epic. One more shot at the elusive brass ring. Could it be possible? Was I fooling myself to even reach for it? Didn't matter. I knew I was going to grasp onto it with both hands, and the teasing from Fiorino be damned. "Where do I sign up?"

CHAPTER THREE

Hannah

I flinched as the bouquet smacked me square in the face and dropped awkwardly into my hands. *Great, just great.* Out of the corner of my eye, I saw my mother clapping with girlish delight and turning to her bridge friends to share her excitement. Instinctively, I grabbed at the offending floral projectile amid mixed squeals of both joy and disappointment from my fellow bridesmaids and Sophia's single girlfriends.

Sophia's toss had gone awry and rebounded off one of the ballroom pillars, sending the damn flowers straight toward me. As if they were on fire, I flung them back into the air, much to the dismay of my maternal parental unit. If looks could kill, I would have been pulverized. More screams erupted from the female entourage gathered around as they dove and jockeyed for the prize. I put a hand to my face where the stem had struck me, hoping it wouldn't leave a mark. Crazy women! They swarmed like sharks in a tank over the thing as it fell back to earth. I hated stupid traditions and this one most of all.

I backed away from the crowd, only to bump into something solid behind me. As I turned in a slow twirl, I again found myself face to face with Russ Pomeroy.

"Nice catch," he said. "Too bad you threw it away. You should never look a gift horse in the mouth, Hanna-bee."

I sniffed and tossed my mane of hair, choosing to ignore his use of my nickname. For now. "I suppose you think you'll do better at catching the garter?" I asked, both embarrassed and annoyed.

Why didn't he just go find the nearest Star Trek convention and hang out with the other males whose IQs exceeded their weight?

"Well, since you're bringing it up," he said, his lips peeling back to reveal his lopsided, gap-toothed grin. "I'm told I'm a very good catch. Why don't you reel me in and find out? No catching of your sister's bridal bouquet needed. I'm a sure thing."

My stomach lurched in revulsion. Swallowing hard to keep the bile from rising in my throat, I gulped in a breath. Yep. Raw meat again. With a tiny shiver, I vowed to become a vegan. I'd never look at animal protein the same way. "Russ, I know you're Phil's brother, and I don't want to cause any family disharmony, but..."

Russ looked at me blankly, his grin fading. "Yes?"

I exhaled the rancid breath stalled in my lungs. "I don't know how else to say this, so I'll just say it. We're never going to be a couple."

Russ looked genuinely shocked. His expression went from benign to almost menacing. I kept going, before I lost my nerve. "You're not my type. I - I'm not your type. And I'm going away to grad school, so I won't be around anyway. Please stop following me. It's creepy."

Russ's brows knit together in anger. "Really?" he said sarcastically. "Well, that explains the bouquet. Looks like you make a habit of throwing away every good chance you get." He leaned in slightly, stabbing his thumb toward his chest. "I'm a respected businessman in this town. You could do worse you know, little Miss I'm-too-good-for-everyone. And just so you know, you're not nearly as pretty as Sophia or Eloise. You'd do well to remember it. You're nothing but the family afterthought."

I winced at his words, moving to apologize when I should reach out and smack him. But he'd hit me in my sore spot, and after all, he was... close to being right. I had been an unplanned pregnancy. "I'm sorry..."

"Forget it," he spat, waving his hand in dismissal. "Who wants a stuck-up chick who had to work her ass off for a lowly B-? Good luck in grad school... maybe it'll make you smarter than you were in college." He turned on his heel and stalked away, his rented tux hanging from his gangly limbs.

Tears stung my eyelids as I watched him go, but for what reasons I wasn't certain. That he'd dissed my intellectual worth? Or that even a guy who sawed cows into steaks for a living wouldn't want me? Mostly because I already had an inferiority complex, and he'd hit me right where it hurt the most.

"Hannah, you okay?" my sister's voice asked from behind.

"Yeah, sure. Why wouldn't I be?" I said, hiding the pain. It had been my modus operandi for so long, deflection forced me to paint a mask on my face.

Eloise stepped close and reached to touch my cheek. "Oh, honey. That must have really hurt."

Not as much as being trash-talked by the biggest loser in town. This must be what Cole feels like when he has a bad game, and the rabid Riot fans suspend their angry limbs from the plexiglass, trying to get to him.

"Nothing Russell Pomeroy could say will ever hurt me," I replied.

More like lied.

El's brilliant green eyes narrowed in concern. "I was talking about the flowers," she said, her gaze flicking to Russ's retreating figure. "What did he say to you? Is he bothering you again? All it would take is one steely glare from The Beantown Bard, and he'd run in the other direction." Eloise craned her neck to search out her husband. I stayed her with a tap on the arm.

"No testosterone needed, El. This is a girl problem." I sighed, collapsing into my sister's arms. "What am I going to do? I can't stay here anymore. I have to leave Columbus."

Eloise drew me as close as she could with her conspicuous baby bump creating a barrier between us. "What do you mean?" she asked, stroking my auburn head that contrasted so distinctly from my sisters' dark brunette tresses. "You're off to grad school in a few weeks. You won't have to see Russ Pomeroy ever again."

"That's just it," I cried. "I'm not going to grad school. At least not to Franklin. Not anywhere. Well, maybe I qualify to work at McDonalds. I didn't get accepted!" My chest caved in and out in sobbing breaths. "I can't re-apply until next term." I looked up with tear-filled eyes. "I haven't told Mom and Dad."

"Oh, Hanna-bee," Eloise crooned. "I'm so sorry. I wish I could help. Do you want me to send Cole down to the admissions office and…"?

"No!" I leaned against Eloise's shoulder. My big sister, the strong one, the one who always knew what to do. I needed her now more than ever, but Eloise had enough on her plate. A new husband and a baby on the way, with a business to run on top of it all. An idea struck me.

"El," I said, my voice pleading. "You *can* help. Take me with you back to Rochester. I can apply to online programs and get a job and…"

El's brow creased. "What?"

My eyes searched hers. "I can work for you in the restaurant. You'll need help with the baby coming, and the precautions you said your doctor wants you to take because it's a high-risk pregnancy. I know you could use the help, El. Please."

"Hold on, slow down," Eloise said, but I wouldn't be stopped.

"I'll tell Mom and Dad that you asked me to come, that you need my help. I can say I deferred grad school until next year, so I could work and earn some money and help you."

"You can't just toss grad school," El said, bracing me by the shoulders. "Education is everything. It's your whole future. You have to tell Mom and Dad the truth. And I'd have to clear it with Cole first."

"I know, I know. But he'll say yes, he'll be back on the ice soon. What if baby comes early, and he's on the road? He'll be happy to know you have me on hand." I straightened and swiped at my eyes, my determination returning. And with it a renewed sense of purpose. This was the perfect solution. A win-win. "You *need* me."

Eloise sighed and brushed a strand of bangs away from my face. "You're right. I do need you. And more importantly, you need me. How can I say no?"

CHAPTER FOUR

Ryder

"You're shitting me," Cole said, adding a low whistle to his statement. "You're gonna try out after all these years? You better pedal faster, old man. You know the median age of the tryouts will be teenagers."

I grinned as I amped up the tension on my spin bike. I didn't mind a little ribbing about my physical condition. I could get in shape, no problem. Fitness was the least of my worries. Though I'd been allowed to use the Riot's training facility during my employment with the club, for the first time, I felt like I truly belonged there. If it took everything I had, I was going to make it to the NHL.

Not one fucking thing could stop me now. Including myself.

"Don't worry about me, Fiorino," I said, glancing at the man out of the corner of my eye. "If you hear footsteps behind you, it's me."

"Ha. In your dreams," Cole said as he mounted the stair climber and began to pump away.

Sweat trickled down my neck and into the crease between my shoulder blades as I pedaled with renewed vigor. My hockey dreams had been given new life, and I'd never felt better or stronger. I reveled in the sights and smells of the workout space – the gleaming chrome and black powdered steel of the machines. My nose settled on the mixed aromas of rubber, vinyl and men's body odor. It didn't bother me in the least. In fact, I found it comforting, even inspiring.

Our first on-ice session would be tomorrow, and I could hardly wait. When I finished my workout, I mopped my face and neck and headed for the showers. I caught my reflection in the mirrors as I undressed and gave myself a fierce and unrelenting physical critique. Had I put on weight since hanging up the blades?

A little, maybe. But hidden beneath the dress shirts and suit jackets of my daily job were sculpted abs, pecs, and deltoids I was proud to call my own. Amber-brown eyes stared back at me from beneath my stylish shock of sandy brown hair. With my good looks, stellar physique, and this gift of a second chance at hockey, nothing would stand in my way again of attaining the life I so desperately wanted and all the trappings that went with it. I smiled in approval.

The holier-than-thou Eloise Fiorinos of the world could go jump in Silver Lake.

CHAPTER FIVE

Hannah

"We're disappointed of course," my dad said in his stern, fatherly voice. "But proud of you for offering to help your sister."

"You've re-submitted your application for grad school at Franklin, haven't you?" my mom added.

"Yes, of course," I lied. I wasn't at all sure I wanted to go to Franklin now, seeing as it meant staying in Columbus. Winona or an online program would be just fine until I got my legs underneath me. But my parents didn't need to know that. Not yet. Not with the promise of escaping to Rochester in my sights. "There's no guarantee they'll accept me next time either. I've heard it's even harder to get in during the middle of the year."

"Nonsense, sweetheart," Mom admonished. "You're a very smart girl. Perhaps you should take some online courses in the meantime."

Did my mother have some kind of freakish sixth sense? If not, she sure as heck had a good radar for the unspoken plans of her three daughters. I glanced at my mom's eager expression. I appreciated the vote of confidence but didn't feel smart at all. Not compared to my overachieving sisters.

"I'm not sure I'll have time," I said. "Maybe once the baby comes?" I hoped the vague, dangling promise would satisfy my mother's wishes.

"Alright," she said, drawing me close to her wide, well-padded frame. "You be good, don't cause any trouble for Eloise and Cole. Eloise is supposed to take it easy and not have any stress."

Had our mother even met her classic, Type A, overachieving daughter lately? Asking Eloise to take it easy would be like a cowboy trying to herd a cat.

"I won't." I traded the embrace for my father's all-encompassing one. Gerry Robertson was a giant of a man, his large limbs seasoned by a lifetime of work in the trades.

"I expect you to work hard out there," he said, his chest rumbling comfortingly against my cheek. "I didn't spend thirty years bolting up pipe to raise a lazy princess. You show El and Cole your A-game."

As I hugged him, I still felt that familiar wave of disapproval from my dad despite his words of encouragement. I always felt I never measured up to my sisters in his eyes, but consciously dismissed the thought as irrational. Fathers always wanted the best for their daughters, especially the youngest of the brood – arriving so many years after Sophia. A mistake that delayed their retirement and subsequent travel. They knew it. I knew it. Even though they would never articulate it.

"I will. I'll be at El's beck and call," I affirmed.

"You'll have a great example to follow," Dad said, his pride in his firstborn never easy to conceal. Now, Eloise would raise even higher on her pedestal as the mother of Dad's first grandchild. I would lay down my life savings against any Vegas odds the unborn Fiorino had a penis.

I sighed as he released me and glanced at Eloise. El answered me with a wink. "Don't worry about Cinderella here, Dad. I'll have her earning her invitation to the ball."

"I'm going to miss you both so much," Sophia said, her tone mournful as she interrupted to add her own farewells. She grabbed El's hand. "You'll let us know the minute you go into labor, right?"

"Of course," El said.

"And you." Sophia turned to me. "You take care of Eloise and the baby." She sniffed and made a pre-emptive swipe to the corner of her eye. "Russ is going to miss you too."

My eyes shot heavenward. "Please. The last thing I care about is Russ Pomeroy's feelings. He's a big, fat, fu…" I caught myself and threw Sophia a look of apology. If I laid down an F-bomb in front of our father, it might earn me a look I wouldn't recover from for days. "No offense to Phil."

"None taken, but I'm the shoulder Russ is going to be crying on. Have sympathy for me at least."

"You've got it," El said.

"In spades," I agreed.

"You could do worse, you know," Dad said as he folded his weathered arms. "Russ is a nice boy with a successful business going. A good provider. And he'd never abuse you."

My heart constricted as I heard Russ's words coming from my father's mouth. Was that the limit of his expectations for me, settle down and marry the wimpy boy next door even though doing so would ensure a life I didn't want? At least my mother seemed to have higher hopes.

I tugged my lower lip between my teeth. "Geez, Dad. Isn't there supposed to be more to life than being able to go out in public with clothes on your back and without a bruise for eye makeup? You'd think we've entered a time machine and gone back to the days of June Cleaver."

"Bye, sisters of mine!" Sophia shouted, interfering with our father's response.

El and I waved to all of them as we stepped into the waiting Town Car.

"Sophia looks happy," I said as the car pulled away, heading for the airport. With cloudy eyes and only a tiny tinge of regret, I watched my childhood home shrink in the distance.

"Ecstatically happy," El agreed.

"Kinda like you," I said, glancing sideways at Eloise. "You have it all. Gorgeous husband, not to mention wealthy. A baby on the way and a thriving business enterprise. Wish I could be as lucky as you and Soph."

El patted her my hand. "You will be. Someday. Give it time. You're still so young, but I see a happy ending in your future."

After we landed in Rochester, Cole met us at the baggage claim, and I could only stare at the man. Of course, I'd met him at their wedding but still felt awestruck in the presence of a bona fide NHL star. I managed to avert my eyes as he took my sister in his arms and kissed her with a gentle fervor that I envied, communicating the deep love and connection they had forged between them. Their unborn child cemented their relationship as no other bond ever could. A selfish wave of jealousy washed over me, and I stiffened in order to keep the frown off my face. Eloise was doing me a favor. I had to buck up.

Cole turned his attention to me, flashing a brilliant smile. "Welcome to Minnesota. I swear you're even prettier than when I saw you last. You'll have to fight off all our male patrons with a hockey stick. Lucky for you, I have a few spares."

"Cole," Eloise admonished. "Don't scare her off the first day, okay? She's going to think we're nothing but barbarians in this frozen tundra."

Cole laughed and wrapped an arm around El's shoulders. "Okay, but a gorgeous redhead in our establishment can only be good for business. They'll be coming back for seconds. And thirds."

I blushed but secretly loved the compliments. My ego could

use a little more of it, that was for sure, especially after the stomping it had been taking recently.

"Hey," Cole continued, "did you hear that the Riot is holding open tryouts for a new player? They'll do evaluations up to Thanksgiving, then make their pick. He'll get some ice time in home games until Christmas break, then the team will offer a one-year contract if they're interested. Crazy, huh?"

"By open tryouts, you mean anyone off the street?" El asked. "That is crazy. The league's never done anything like that before. I can't believe Sheehan is going for it."

Cole held up an index finger. "Going for it. That wily old bastard masterminded the whole damn thing. And as far as being crazy, I'm not so sure. Major league baseball did it once a few years back, so there's precedent. I'm thinking of hosting a party at Casa Fiorino for whoever the new recruit happens to be. Make it a fundraiser for youth hockey here in Rochester. You know how much I love raising money for underprivileged kids so they can play. What do you think?"

El drew in a big breath as we began moving toward our baggage carousel. "I think Hannah and I have a lot of work ahead of us."

Cole snapped his fingers and winked at me. If he wasn't my brother-in-law, I'd let my mouth hang open so the drool could escape. With his black hair and blue eyes, Cole gave new meaning to the word dreamy.

"Oh, by the way," he said with his trademark grin. "I have a confession to make about Sophia's cake. I had a bite before I had to catch the red-eye to make my pre-camp drills the next day."

Eloise reared back, a look of question lighting her eyes. "What about the cake? Lucinda's bakery was in charge of it. I thought it was beautiful."

"Negative, wife. Dry. Dry as a bone. Dry as the Sahara. Dry as..."

"I get the point," Eloise moaned. "You've been so spoiled by your mother's cooking that nothing short of perfection meets with your satisfaction. I'll admit. It was a little dry."

"Now, wouldn't my fine Italian mama's tiramisu be far more palatable? With a side of powdered sugar delight?" Cole asked, his hand sneaking downward to pinch El's rear end. Eloise flinched and playfully slapped his hand away. "Nothing could match that fantastic donut-tower cake, babes."

"True," she acknowledged with a tilt of her head. "Sorry you had to leave to make it to pre-camp. It would seem that your new coach is going to be a hard taskmaster."

"Yup. Nothing I can't handle. If he rides my ass, I'll write my next soliloquy in his honor."

El looked him over, the love and desire she felt for her husband plain to see. "I chose a life with you. I won't ever be jealous of your career taking first place, you know that. I've learned to live with it."

"I know," he said with a grin. "You're the best wife ever, and you're about to become the best mom ever. To little Cole, Jr."

I felt a little like a third wheel in the unfolding scenario. The loveless, wide-eyed, pain in the ass little sister. Tagging along again, just as I'd done as a child. Maybe this had all been a really bad idea. I cleared my throat to remind them of my presence.

El's gaze snapped to me. "Sorry, Hanna-bee. You'll have to excuse us newlyweds."

I flashed a forgiving smile. "I'll learn to live with it."

***

The décor of Casa Fiorino exuded Tuscan charm. Cole had told me that other than the complex, industrial grade coffee machines which he refused to part with, the tin-paneled ceiling was the only remnant of the building's former coffeehouse chic. I admired the white Venetian plaster walls, finished with a fine gold-leaf over brush that evoked old-world allure. In contrast, modern pieces from Italian artists hung on them. Potted dwarf pine trees dotted the room, and instead of the ubiquitous checkered linens typical of Italian restaurants, forest green tablecloths covered the mix of round, square and rectangular shaped tables. Apparently, Mama Fiorino had insisted the restaurant not resemble a mafia den.

I'd never waited tables before. In fact, I'd never worked before, not even part-time in high school or college. Between grants, loans, and my parent's college accounts, all three Robertson girls had been allowed the luxury of focusing exclusively on their studies. With a pang of irony, I realized my father's cracks about princesses weren't all that far off the mark when it came to me. With the memorized greeting scrolling in my head, I summoned my courage, stacked four menus in the crook of my arm and marched toward the group seated in my section.

"Hi, welcome to Casa Fiorino," I said as I reached the table. "I'm Hannah, and I'll be your server this evening."

The burly patron looked me up and down, clearly appreciating the view. "It's my lucky day, then," he said with a leering grin. I suppressed a smirk as I saw his girlfriend kick him under the table, his wince of pain my only satisfaction. In the short time I'd been working at the restaurant, I'd become very aware of the effect my appearance had on most men. But it never seemed to mean much beyond the surface ogling. I felt like a dessert that men drooled over on the menu, with no real intent of ever ordering, let alone taking a bite. Not that I'd want this overweight brute. The girlfriend had nothing to worry about.

"Can I start you off with something to drink? Our bar has excellent signature cocktails tonight," I asked, placing a menu in front of each guest. When they'd ordered, I returned to the serving station where Spencer 'Spud' Davies waited behind the bar. "One Sam Adams and three Jack and Cokes. I tried to push the Chamomile Honey and Murphy Whiskey, but it was a no go. They're pretty vanilla."

"You seem to be getting the hang of this," the portly Spud said with a smile, pulling glasses from a rack behind him. He was such a sweetheart, I almost wished I found him attractive.

"I hope so," I answered with a sigh. "My future depends on it."

Spud gave me a curious look. "How so?"

I lifted my gaze toward the filigree ceiling. "If I don't get this right, it's back to Ohio for me. And a short leash."

"You make it sound like jail," Spud chuckled.

I joined in the laugh. "Well, a kind of prison anyway. And it's called Mrs. Robertson. Not Mrs. *Robin*son. The latter lady had to be a lot more fun than my mother."

"Can't be all that bad," Spud said. "But hey, maybe the man of your dreams will walk into Casa Fiorino someday and take you away from all this." He winked and gave a slight jerk of his chin toward my table.

I glanced at the scruffy boyfriend still leering at my ass in my tight black uniform pants. After imagining Russ Pomeroy's head stuck on his stocky body, I cringed. No. That would not be my future.

No. Fucking. Way.

"I never went to grad school," Spud continued, "and look how I turned out." He rubbed his ample belly. "You might want to re-think that school plan." He smiled as he filled my tray with the drink order. "It's expensive, and half your life will be over before you're even done."

I covered up my grimace with a wry grin. So this is what it came down to. Advice from a bartender. Oh well, they were supposed to be good at that, weren't they? I offered Spud my best smile. The same one I wouldn't be giving to the customer with the lurid stares. "Thanks."

With my spirits drooping, I carried the tray to my customer's table, pasting a pleasant expression on my face that I hoped wouldn't crack and fall off like dried Kabuki makeup. As I took the group's meal orders, Spud's words echoed in my head. Maybe this was a mistake, after all. I'd guilted my own sister into rescuing me, giving me a job. All I'd really done was run away from reality. From the frying pan into the fire. No Prince Charming was likely to rescue me anytime soon and let me avoid facing my own future. Maybe I should go back to Columbus and slay my own dragons.

But I couldn't leave now. The big holiday fundraiser loomed on the calendar, and so did Eloise's due date. So far, her pregnancy hadn't presented any complications, but El's medical history left room for concern. I'd thought being grown up would mean freedom, but all it really meant was responsibility. With a capital R.

"Thank you," I said as I gathered up the menus. Perhaps by some miracle, my dream man could walk through the doors of Casa Fiorino one day. Perhaps R could also stand for Romance. After all, fairy tales were for princesses locked in towers. And I'd be waiting right here in this one.

CHAPTER SIX

Ryder

The sweet 'ping' of the metal bar sounded like music to my ears. My shot ricocheted into the back of the net like a stray bullet, straight over the shoulder of the Riot's backup goalie, Jim Bennett. A whooping shout left my lips as I raised my stick and skated around the boards in triumph.

The drills and conditioning had all come back to me in the past six weeks. Just like riding a bike. The thrill of being on the ice again, sucking lungfuls of frosty air and feeling the sweat collect under my pads exhilarated me like nothing else in the world. I felt like I could do anything – move mountains with a flick of my blade or lift a car off an accident victim with one hand.

I was unstoppable.

Cole Fiorino skated up behind me as we queued up to repeat the drill pattern. We'd become closer friends since working through the tryouts, still rivals in a sense but the jealousy I felt toward Cole had dissipated as well as the vitriol I garnered for the man's wife. I realized the weight of those feelings all these years had held me down, embittered me, and made me a lesser man than I could be. If I harbored regrets in my life, these were surely at the top of the list.

And with this new opportunity looming, I'd decided to work over my entire life in the process.

"Nice shot," Cole said, then changed his tone to a falsetto squeak. "You still got it, Betty... boop boop be doop!"

"Footsteps, bro. Footsteps," I taunted him.

Cole shook his head. "The only footsteps I'm going to hear are the patter of little feet in a few months. My *son's*."

I nodded but kept my focus on the ice in front of me. "Congrats, man. I didn't know you were having a boy."

A grin curled his lips. "I don't really know yet. But somehow, I *know*. Sorry, hard for me not to brag. I forgot that you—"

I snorted a laugh. "Forget it. Ancient history. As for the Betty Boop comment, that catalog should be arriving in the mail any day now."

After flashing a broad smile, I skated off to begin the drill again. I'd joked with Cole about a fictional catalog of hockey wife candidates that was distributed to all NHL players. Now that I was literally close enough to smell the Riot's locker room, I no longer had an interest in ice queens like the new Mrs. Fiorino. But maybe a real relationship with a woman who was more my type. I'd tried to fit a square peg into a round hole and so had she. Lesson learned.

Why didn't loose chicks hold much interest for me anymore? I shook my head – I'd worry about it later along with making over my entire life. Right now, I needed to be laser focused on making the team and not let hot chicks disturb my flow.

I worked my way through the series of pylons, my puck handling feeling natural and swift, like I'd never been away from the game. My rec team had kept me in tune, but those hacks would never recognize me now. As my speed and game sense heightened, I'd made the first three cuts in the tryouts. My confidence was soaring to new heights, pushing the weight of self-doubt off my shoulders. The number of contenders for the coveted spot on the Riot's roster was down to only two players: me as a defenseman, and a smaller forward who no one seemed to know – Joe Thibault. Soon, it would be one. And

I intended to be the last man standing.

When the session ended, I showered and changed back into my suit and tie. It was still a workday, and my boss, Kristoff Helios, hadn't exactly given his blessing for me to participate in the tryouts. As marketing manager, Kristoff had prior knowledge of the impending publicity move, and though it was his job to promote it, didn't see its value in boosting sales. Potentially losing one of his top sales reps as a result irritated the man even further.

I settled in behind my desk, my mind and body still on a high from the endorphins cycling through me. I hoped it wouldn't be long before I could leave its shiny surface littered with memos and promotional literature far behind, along with every other unpleasant memory stored in my brain. With a groan, I leaned back as Kristoff headed toward me. I moved to pick up my desk phone and feign a dummy call when my personal cell buzzed in my breast pocket.

Throwing Kristoff a helpless look, I grabbed for the device, halting the arrogant man's advance partway across the carpeted floor. "This is Ryder," I answered without looking at the screen.

"About damn time," came a graveled voice over the connection. My blood drained into my toes, the drop in pressure cementing my lower body into my leather desk chair. Unable to move, to think. "Why didn't you answer your goddamn phone before?"

I hadn't noticed the missed calls in my scramble to avoid Kristoff's approach and the resulting lecture. Jesus, this was the last person I'd expected to hear from. And it sure as hell wasn't Jesus. *Not now. Not when things are taking a turn for the better.* I swiveled my chair toward the wall of my cubicle so my voice wouldn't carry. "Dad?"

"Yeah, it's me, dipshit. Who'd you think it'd be, Saint fucking Nicholas? Complete with a red velvet sack of gifts for your worthless ass."

A long pause. "Where are you?"

A rough grunt issued from his throat. "Right where you left me. In the joint." I swallowed hard. It was no one's fault but my father's as to why he'd landed in prison. No words lingered on my tongue appropriate for work. "But not for much longer, if you get your candy ass out here to pick me up. I'm out on Thursday. Parole board wants my ugly mug outta here. I'll expect to see you waiting outside the exit gate for your dear ol' dad. In your expensive ride."

Panic crawled up my neck, threatening to choke me. The old man was out, and with his older brothers both out of the country, I was his last resort. The day he'd left for the penitentiary, hadn't been a good one. I still had nightmares a few times a month, waking up in a cold sweat and unable to get back to sleep.

"That so," I muttered, not inviting further discourse. I'd never wanted anything so badly as to hang up at that moment. Except getting an NHL contract. And I refused to let this alcoholic bastard fuck that up.

"Well? You gonna be there or not?" he growled, then coughed.

I ground my teeth. "Where am I supposed to take you? Your house got auctioned off in the foreclosure years ago." I dreaded the answer I already knew was coming.

"You have a fancy-ass apartment in Rochester, don't you? I got no place else to go."

CHAPTER SEVEN

Hannah

"You shouldn't be doing that!" I exclaimed, rushing to my sister's aid. I laid my hands on the cardboard box that Eloise had lifted off the delivery pallet. "For heaven's sake, El, do you want to give birth right here in cold storage?"

"Don't be such an alarmist," Eloise scoffed. "I feel perfectly fine."

Would my sister ever stop trying to do everything herself? After a tense moment, she released the package to my outstretched arms with a long-suffering sigh and a dramatic eye roll. She straightened, putting one hand on her back and the other on her protruding abdomen. Her face creased in discomfort.

"See? That's why I'm here," I scolded, placing the box on a metal shelf. "To stop you from trying to do everything yourself, like you always have." I took Eloise by the elbow and led her into the gleaming warmth of Casa Fiorino's kitchen. "Let somebody else take charge for a change. Don't you dare put yourself and my future niece or nephew at risk, especially not over a twenty-pound box of lamb chops!" I seated Eloise in a chair and shook my pointer finger in my sister's puffy face.

"Hanna-bee, you are becoming a certified tyrant," Eloise said with a weak laugh, still rubbing her belly and wincing in pain. "Guess I'm not used to taking orders. You kind of remind me of myself."

"You know what your doctor said," I stated, one hip jutting

out. "With your gynecological history, the chances of early delivery are high. It's nearly Thanksgiving, the fundraiser's next week, and your due date is only a few months away. Are you trying to get an early Christmas present for yourself? One that's wanted but not until it's fully incubated?"

Eloise smiled. "Maybe he or she will be born on my birthday, the sixteenth. That'd be convenient. The sooner the better, I say. I hate taking things easy. I hate rolling around here like an overinflated beach ball. I hate not being able to ask my hot husband to ravish my naked body. I—"

I put my hands over my ears. "Ew, too much information. Just this once, El, quit trying to control everything, okay?"

Uncharacteristically, Eloise seemed to give up and relax in her chair. "Okay."

I nodded in satisfaction. "Okay. Now, we were going to go over the checklist for the fundraiser. I'll get it."

"Wow, you really can be an ogre when you want to be." Eloise chuckled. "Wanna-bee. You're becoming more like my clone daily. I bow down. Too bad Dad's not here to see it and grunt his approval."

I would ordinarily have chafed at that name, but since I finally had the upper hand over big sis, I could only laugh. "According to Dad, I'm a princess." I made a leering face and held my hands up, fingers wiggling. "Just call me Fiona, and I can be a little bit green-faced ogre and diamond tiara-wearer all at the same time."

After retrieving El's tablet from the adjoining office, I pulled up a chair next to her. "Menu... check. Liquor delivery... check. Decorating crew... that'd be me... check. Silent auction items... fifty and counting." I looked up. "Ticket sales?"

Eloise lifted a shoulder. "That's Cole's department."

I blinked in disbelief. "You let a man be in charge of

something that important? What if no one shows up? That would be a disaster."

El tossed her hands up. "He's all over it. He has all the contacts with the team, and he's the face of hockey in this town."

I bit my lower lip, picturing an empty restaurant and a low donation. "Has he sold any yet?"

Eloise frowned, clearly not wanting to answer. "I don't know."

I flipped the cover on the tablet. "Well, we'd better ask him then, shouldn't we?"

Eloise touched the screen on her cell phone and handed it over. "Be my guest. It will be better coming from you anyway. If you haven't noticed, he has a soft spot."

I watched Eloise as I waited for the call to connect. I didn't like that grey cast on her skin, and the discomfort she wasn't hiding well… at least not from someone who'd known her all her life.

"Hey, PDL. What's up," Cole's voice said in a rush, using his nickname for Eloise, Pretty Donut Lady. He sounded anxious. I guessed that any time a man got a call from his very pregnant wife, he would be snapping to attention.

I twirled a lock of long hair around my finger. "Wrong. It's Hannah, I'm using El's phone."

"What, what's happening?" His voice rose to a high-pitched squeal. He sounded like a piglet wiggling away from a farmer's grip. "Is El alright?"

"Yes, yes. She's right here. We're just being proactive about the fundraiser. How are the ticket sales coming? We're counting on you, brother-in-law."

A hiss ripped through the line. "Jeez, don't scare me like that. I thought the time had come, and I stink so bad I'd have to creep up on my bathwater."

I wrinkled my nose. "Sorry, sounds like a personal problem to me. So about the tickets?"

A pause. "Tickets... yeah. Uh, with all the extra ice time I guess I forgot. I'll get on it. I'll get one of the guys to help out."

I stomped a foot on the floor, sending up a little cloud of flower. "Cole! The party's next week! Doesn't the club have a marketing team? Why aren't they flogging the hell out of this?"

"Well, it's a private function, but you just gave me an idea. I know just the guy for the job. Let me talk to Eloise."

"Okay, here she is."

Handing the phone back to El, I crossed my arms and observed my sister even more closely. Something didn't seem right. Instead of radiant, Eloise seemed tired and pale. A little inner voice told me that Hanna-bee needed to stick close to the hive. The Queen Bee might need a little more help than she was letting on.

***

"Where are those bid sheets?" I called to the back office.

"Just printing them off now," Eloise answered. I surveyed the display of donated items I'd arranged in a back section of the restaurant and nodded in satisfaction. The community had been very generous. Everything from game tickets to ski packages to power tools. If the bidding was fierce, we'd net a good profit next Friday night, and all of it would go to kids' hockey programs around the city. Though I had only a passing interest in hockey, I felt proud of what we'd accomplished and the good it would do in the community. And Cole would be over the moon. He coached some of the youth during the offseason at the Rochester Community Center's indoor rink with the help of his huge goalie friend, Shredder. I dusted my hands on my jeans and strode into the office.

"Here they are," El said, handing me a neat stack of sheets still warm from her desktop printer.

"Great." I took the papers and smiled at Eloise. "I think we're ready."

Eloise returned the smile. "You've done a great job helping organize this event. I couldn't have pulled it off without you. You make a great manager. Maybe you ought to think about a degree in hospitality or event management."

Taking an exaggerated breath, I brushed my fingernails on my inflated chest. "I'm just trying to be helpful. Earn my keep, you know. Make the old man proud."

Eloise pushed back from her desk, which wasn't a far distance since she couldn't sit as close to it as usual with her swollen belly. "You've earned more than your keep. I'm so grateful that you're here. You surprise me, Hanna-bee. I'd never have thought you had so much strength in you. You've been my rock."

I leaned down to give Eloise a one-armed hug. "I thought that's what husbands were supposed to be, but I'm glad to help." I patted my sister's shoulder. "It must be hard being married to a guy who isn't around much. I don't think I could handle being a hockey wife. When I get married, I want a guy who worships the ground I walk on. One who rushes home from the office every night just to be near me and breathe the same air."

Eloise looked at me, one eyebrow raised. "Have you been reading those paperback romances again? Love doesn't go by the book, just so you know. It can hide, it can run away, masquerade as something else and then one day sneak up on you when you're not looking."

My eyes widened into moons. "Is that how it happened for you?"

El grinned and looked away for a moment, her gaze distant. "It plays games too. Like rock-paper-scissors."

"What?" I asked, confusion fogging my brain.

Eloise re-focused on me. "My point is, when love finds you, your brain will hand over the reins to your heart. You'll stop analyzing and throw that list of qualifications out the window. You won't care if he's an athlete or an ant farmer. It'll just work. You mark my words, Hanna-bee, it will hit you in the solar plexus just like a wrecking ball."

CHAPTER EIGHT

Ryder

"Yo, Ryder!" Cole shouted amid the din inside the dressing room. Men were slobs, and professional athletes weren't much better. Gear and clothing items presented an obstacle course between us, and Cole had to pick his way through.

Already on my way out with my bag on my shoulder, I stopped in the doorway and turned. "What's up?"

"What's your hurry?" Cole asked, gesturing to my fully dressed state. "Part of the experience is hanging with the team."

I gave a condescending nod. "Some of us have real jobs, you know. I can't hang, or I'll be fired by my nemesis... er, boss, Kristoff Helios. Ever heard of him?"

Cole grinned and caught up to me in a few strides, still wearing his skates. "Yeah, El's mentioned him once or twice. She's not a fan. And I'm not happy he's had his moldy cock inside *my* wife. But maybe you won't have to deal with that douche for much longer. Gotta tell ya, I'm impressed. I didn't realize you'd kept in such good shape. I think the club's close to making their decision."

I waved my free hand, a jolt of unease splitting my confidence in half. "Don't jinx it, man. Let the chips fall where they may."

Cole reached out for a fist bump. "Hey, credit where credit is due. If you've got the skills, luck has nothing to do with it."

I pursed my lips, suspicious of Cole's sudden interest.

"Thanks for the pep talk. Gotta go."

"Wait, you know I'm setting up an event at the restaurant, to introduce our new player to the city. A fundraiser for youth hockey in Rochester. It's really close to my heart, man."

I nodded. "Yeah. I heard."

He scrubbed a hand down his scruffy beard. "Well, I kinda dropped the ball in selling tickets. Since you're technically still in sales, think you could flog a few? It would mean the world to me, and with El about to explode with our baby, I'm kind of in a shitstorm. We're planning on honoring the winner of the contest that night."

My eyebrows shot up. Even though me and Cole had propagated some quasi-bromance while on the ice, Cole Fiorino still had everything I wanted, including the girl. The pregnant girl. The last thing I wanted was spending my very limited down time doing the heir apparent a favor. "Kinda self-serving of me, don't you think? Not to mention awkward. They could still pick the other guy."

Cole shook his head. "I don't think so. And you'd want your family there, wouldn't you? You have parents in the area, right? And a couple of brothers, as I recall."

The comment took me by surprise, but I didn't correct Cole. I didn't want to talk about my deceased mother or my drunken father. The dude had a long memory. Maybe he wasn't such an arrogant, self-centered pain in the ass. So much had changed since juniors. I guess I needed to cut Fiorino more slack – myself too for that matter. "C'mon, you know how important the minor system is. Neither of us would be here if we hadn't been given a chance to play as kids."

"Sure," I agreed after a moment. "Consider them sold. Since it's for kids, after all."

"Thanks, man. I know you'll want as many eyeballs there as

possible when Rochester meets the Riot's newest member."
Cole punched me on the arm.

I could only nod and move on. My thoughts were elsewhere than Cole's fundraiser. As focused as I needed to be on my performance in the tryouts, another crisis required my attention. The comments about my family ripped through me like a rusted knife. And just as toxic. Cole didn't know that Joan Martin had passed away from cancer ten years earlier. Didn't know that my brothers had taken off as soon as they'd graduated, taking jobs overseas – as far away from our hometown and our abusive father as they could get. How could he? He hadn't kept in touch.

And I didn't make a habit of advertising that my father was serving an eight-year sentence for criminal negligence. He was the last person I would want in attendance at my long awaited and hard-earned moment of glory. I dreaded the drive out to Rochester FMC. Even more, I dreaded the prospect of being in my father's company. Most likely listening to his diatribe on how the union had fucked him over, didn't protect him after the incident. Talk about a man who didn't want to take accountability. I wanted to point out to the old man that when you were always the person at the scene of every crime, that was a growth opportunity.

I'd have to find the old man a place to stay, fast. The idea of having him bunk in at my apartment caused nausea to lick the back of my throat. I didn't need this extra stress – not now. Not ever. My anxiety gave way to anger. What did the world have against me? When opportunity finally knocked, why was my alcoholic father's shadow hanging over the doorway?

***

"Hmm, just like I thought. Some white-collar yuppie's gay-ass pad," Dad grunted as he looked around the room, breathing heavily from our climb up the stairs to my second-floor walk-up. I'd chosen it for its historic charm and as an excuse to keep myself in shape by force. Climbing the stairs multiple times a day was good for the old ticker as well as the leg muscles.

My eyes narrowed, gazing at the crown moldings, stained glass inserts and exposed brick through my father's rustic eyes. "Yeah, well. It's better than the Mission Street shelter. Which is where you'll be going next if you're gonna talk shit like that. You're welcome, by the way."

He tossed his duffle bag down with a whump. His civilian clothes were ill-fitting and out of style but were all he had for the time being. If my old man thought I was going to spring for some fancy new duds, he was sorely mistaken. The fucking gravy train had pulled out of the station.

I wondered what it would be like to actually have a father that gave a shit. Like Cole's. Or even Shredder's who was a motherfucking billionaire. One that stepped up to the plate to provide instead of the other way around. I felt like I'd stepped into an alternate universe where I was the victim of some random role reversal. If I wanted to be a father, I'd knock up some loose broad which would be a lot more fun than this shit. My eyes scanned his frail body. The older man had lost a lot of weight since he'd been behind bars.

He cleared his throat. "I suppose I should thank you."

I snorted and walked to the galley-style kitchen. "I gotta get back to the office. There's food in the fridge. And don't bother to look for booze. There isn't any."

"You don't drink?" He eyed me suspiciously. "Since when?"

"Didn't say I didn't drink. Just not here. And not with you."

My father stomped his foot on the hardwood. "Some host you are."

"Door's behind you," I said. "Nothing stopping you from leaving."

"Yeah, yeah, okay. I get it. I'm persona non grata. Just give me a few days to figure things out, then I'll be out of your sissy GQ hair." My dad slumped into an oversized leather armchair near the window.

"What's your plan?" I asked. "I doubt they'll let you back on a job site."

His stubby fingers groped for the remote to my 72-inch plasma. "I wouldn't even if they did, so don't get your panties in a wad. None of your concern."

I curled my hands into fists. "It is if you think you're going to hole up here for a while. I don't want any illegal activities to be even remotely associated with my apartment. Or me."

"I'll make my way. And not the easy way, like you," he said, pointing a finger at me.

I zipped up my jacket and prepared to leave, holding my rising ire in check. Yeah, dealing with Kristoff and his constant irrational demands and temper was *easy*. "Nothing easy about college. I graduated with honors, by the way. Not that you were around to see it."

"You only finished school because you didn't make it in hockey. You had the talent, just not the drive. You were lazy. You were so fucking lazy you put popcorn in your pancakes, so they'd turn over by themselves."

I kept my tight fists stuck to my pants to keep from reaching for my father and wringing his scrawny neck. How dare he? "At least I didn't kill anybody," I muttered, wanting to start screaming for the satisfaction of railing at him. More than that, I wanted to get the hell away from him and starting World War III wouldn't allow for escape.

"You fucking little shit," he spat, rising from his chair. He seemed to wheeze with the effort. Even at his full height, I towered over him. "That fitter took those bolts off himself, not me. It was his own fault. Didn't know enough to check that the line was depressurized."

"You were the foreman. It was your job to check. You were drunk." I couldn't help myself and shot the verbal barb straight for my father's heart.

Direct hit.

"I was not!" he fumed. "Yeah, I'd had drinks that day, but I wasn't drunk when it happened."

I held up a palm between us. "Of course not. You're what's called a functioning alcoholic. Lucky they weren't random testing that day. It would take a five-gallon pail of booze to even show on you, but you were impaired just the same. A man is dead because of you."

My father stepped back, blinking. "You think I don't regret it? I've spent eight years paying for it. You can't know what it was like, seeing that flange explode off the end of that pipe. A cannonball at point-blank range couldn't have done more damage. Crushed him like a walnut." He drew in a rasping breath. "You weren't there."

"Neither was your local, were they?" I finished. "You were so pro-union until then. Where were they when you needed them? They hung you out to dry to save their lily-white asses. Don't lecture me about my choices or my drive. I did just fine without the trades, without the unions. Without you." After gulping a breath, I moved to the door. "Don't wreck anything while I'm gone," I shot over my shoulder, slamming the door behind me.

No way would I share my good news about the Riot with that asshole. With any luck, my unwanted house guest would be gone before Thanksgiving. And for that, I'd give thanks.

CHAPTER NINE

Ryder

The man with the puck accelerated toward me with a full head of steam. I faced him while skating backward, staying with him until the right moment, eyes on the team logo in the center of his chest, not on the puck. It wasn't important. The puck had only two destinations once I made my move. The tiny black disc would land either on my tape or that of one of my teammates. Either way, the skater would give it up and lose the shot opportunity.

I swept my stick in front of me, to knock the puck away from my opponent. The man tried to cut around me but was too close. I nailed him as he tried to pass, the puck bobbing loose as he went down hard on the ice. My linemate scooped up the rubber and sent it swiftly back to the neutral zone in a precision pass to our speedy forward hopeful, Thibault. I heard the thundering of sticks pounding the boards outside the bench, acknowledging my timely hit but didn't stop to bask in the accolades. I followed Thibault and the other forwards into the attacking zone, taking my position at the blue line.

A hard shot from the point rebounded loudly off the pads of Shredder Politski, starting goalie and future hall of famer, the noise like a sonic boom. The rebound rifled back into play, the forwards scrambling to get a stick on it. Without a clear lane, they dug it loose and fired it back to the defense opposite me. My d-partner quickly passed it across, and I wound up my hundred mile per hour slapshot like a coil spring as I watched it sail toward me, unleashing the one-timer with everything I had.

Shouts echoed in the cavern of ice as the puck streaked under the crossbar and popped Shredder's water bottle into the air.

Sniped.

Before I had time to celly, McTaggart's whistle called the entire team to the bench, signaling the end of our inter-squad scrimmage. I couldn't have asked for a better capper to my last on-ice session before the final cut and hoped it would be enough to edge out the competition. Offensive minded defensemen who could put points on the board were worth their weight in gold in the NHL and McTaggart knew the score.

"Great work today, guys," Coach said. "I appreciate the extra time you've all given in between regular games to support this *novelty* tryout initiative. All the other participating teams will have also narrowed their candidate lists to two players. The coaching staff and executives will deliberate over the Thanksgiving holiday and will be contacting both players with a decision and de-briefing on Monday. The successful candidate will see some ice time in our December home games, and contract offerings, if any, will be issued on New Year's Day."

The players rumbled and tapped their sticks on the ice in applause.

With a wave of his hand, he continued, "Remember, the contract is only extended at the discretion of the club management, and all selected players are eligible for trade to another participating team should they be requested. So, Happy Holidays, and don't forget that our very own Mr. Fiorino is hosting a fundraiser next week at his restaurant in support of youth hockey. Hope to see you all there. Now, let's have a round of applause for Martin and Thibault. They both worked hard to get here. May the best man win," Shane finished, a broad smile on his rugged, tanned face.

The Riot's standard cheer rose into the chilled air as they congratulated the potential new players. I watched my competition step off the ice and through the gate. Tiny Thibault, they'd begun to call him. What was the story on this guy? No one had even seen him in the dressing room. He was fast but small – hardly the type to bolster the Riot's physical ice presence.

Cole skated up next to me as the team exited the rink. "How do you feel? Ready for this?"

I pulled off my helmet and gave him a knowing stare. "I've been ready for this my whole life. The league just wasn't ready for me apparently."

Cole tapped me on the back. "You left it all on the ice, bro. Can't ask any more than that."

I nodded. There was no shame in my game, because I'd done just that and now it was out of my hands. "Just hope they're looking for size and a killer shot from the point, and not Speedy Gonzales."

Cole spread his arms wide in a grandiose gesture. "Murphy's got me. Why would he need another forward? What he needs is more protection. For *me*."

"Ego, much?" I snickered, bopping him on the shoulder.

***

I wasn't much of a cook, but I did my best to make a Thanksgiving dinner out of a roasted chicken from the local deli and a trip to the supermarket for potatoes and greens. Better to put up with my father's company in the privacy of my home than worry about him causing a spectacle in some cheesy buffet lineup filled with pressed turkey and Stove Top Stuffing. At least this way I could control the quality of food I put in my body. I had to remain in top condition for what I hoped lay ahead.

My father shifted his sitting position and turned his face from the football on TV long enough to complain. "Are we at least having wine with this feast you're preparing?"

I rammed the potato masher into the pot full of boiled spuds. Addictions died hard. "Yup. The finest de-alcoholized, organic Merlot money can buy."

My dad snorted. "Fuck, boy. Are you trying to kill me?"

Don't give me any ideas, old man. "No. Trying to keep you alive long enough so that you can die somewhere else besides my living room."

A long silence hung in the air before he spoke. "Careful what you wish for. I'll be gone soon enough."

I almost felt sorry for what I'd just said. Almost. "Does that mean you've found a place to live?"

A welcome pause. "It means I've found a place to die."

I stopped punishing my potatoes for a strangled heartbeat. "What are you talking about? If you'd just dry out and get your shit together, everything would be fine. Stop acting like a martyr."

He hoisted himself from the big armchair and shuffled over to the kitchen. "Let me help you with all this," he said, taking the platter of chicken and the salad bowl to the table in the dining nook. "There's a reason I was sent to Rochester FMC. It's a medical facility for inmates, didn't you know?"

I followed with the bowl of mashed potatoes. "Looks like you didn't take advantage of the substance abuse program."

He looked at me with a gentleness in his eyes that took me by surprise. This time I did regret my words.

My father released a breath. "You know why I started drinking. After I lost your mother."

"We all lost mom. You, me, Braden, and Colt. We didn't drown our sorrows in a bottle, and your drinking career started way before that. The day Mom died was just your break-out role."

My father grimaced and looked away. "Yeah. Well, it wasn't the booze they were treating me for. It's mesothelioma. Late onset. Job related." Then he actually smiled. "You're in luck. Today you can give thanks that your old man's going to kick the proverbial bucket soon and be out of your perfectly coiffed hair."

CHAPTER TEN

Hannah

Theresa Fiorino certainly knew how to make an entrance. She stood nearly five-ten in heels, and her fur stole with its matching hat evoked a nineteen forties retro elegance. The older woman's jet-black hair with streaks of gray lay perfectly coifed beneath the fur-trimmed chapeau, and her wide brown eyes set above her regal hooked nose took in every detail of the interior of Casa Fiorino before coming to rest on Eloise.

She spoke one word. "Bella."

Cole smiled. "You like it? Wait 'til you see the kitchen! It's downright inspiring!"

Theresa smiled at her firstborn as he stood next to El. "Yes, darling, it's magnifico, but I was talking about your beautiful wife," she said in the raspy, contralto voice that Cole had perfectly mimicked in the past. She reached a gloved hand to touch Eloise's rounded belly. "Your stunning wife and my equally stunning grandson. You look wonderful, my dear. So glowy. I'm so happy for the two of you."

El shot Cole a look. It seemed all his predictions of a male baby had rubbed off on everyone. I chuckled and tried to hide my smile.

El gripped her mother-in-law's fingers. "Thank you, Theresa. I'm so glad you're able to share Thanksgiving with us."

"You look ready for a dog sled race, Mom," Cole said, gesturing to the furry apparel. "It's not that cold yet." He moved to help her with her coat. "I know people describe

Minnesota as the worst kind of frozen polar ice cap, but it's really not that much different than back home."

Theresa's smile reached every corner of her classic features, adding a merry crinkle around her eyes. "Can we do that? A dog sled race? Sounds exciting!"

Cole laughed. "My mom the thrill seeker," he joked. "What would Dad say?"

"Why do you think he's not here?" Theresa chuckled. "He's turning into a regular fuddy-duddy."

I liked the woman immediately, because I could see the vivacious and mischievous girl behind the striking, mature exterior. Her gaze fell on me. "And who is this stunning angel?" she asked with eyes twinkling. "An actress? No, no. A super model!"

"This is my youngest sister, Hannah," El supplied. "You met her at our wedding, I'm sure. She was one of my bridesmaids."

"Hi," I said, blushing slightly. "I probably looked a little different then."

"I must have been blinded by happiness to not have noticed you," Theresa said, offering her hand to me. "How are you, my dear? Are you living here in Rochester now?"

"Fine, thank you. I'm just out here to help Eloise until the baby comes." *And hopefully forever.* I couldn't believe how much I loved Rochester and how well I fit into the tight-knit community.

"How nice. I'm so glad Eloise is being forced not to overdo it." Theresa turned to Cole. "I hope you've not changed any of my recipes, Coleman Arthur Fiorino. Your grandmother will be cursing you from the grave if you have. And you remember your Nonna. You would never want to be the recipient of one of her... curses."

He threw up a huge hand like an oath. "I wouldn't dare

change anything, but you'll have to be the judge, Mom. Come meet our chef."

The trio continued on their tour of the restaurant while I returned to the long table I'd been setting for the occasion. The kitchen in Eloise's condo wasn't big enough to handle a family dinner party, so we'd opted to have the big Thanksgiving smorgasbord here. Cole and El had been looking for a house to buy in suburban Rochester for some time, but inventory for high-end houses was low, and the right one just hadn't come on the market. After the baby came and everything went back to some semblance of normal, Cole said he might start looking at acreage lots for a new build.

I'd spent a day and a half festooning Casa Fiorino's dining room with holiday swags, wreaths, and poinsettias, and thought it looked exquisite – really festive. As I arranged the napkins in one of the fancy folds I'd learned watching YouTube videos, it struck me that I'd been in Rochester nearly three weeks now. Though I was happy to help my sister, what had I accomplished other than becoming an efficient restaurant worker, sisterly protector, and general gofer? When the baby arrived, space at the condo would be tighter than ever, and my folks were planning to come visit over Christmas too. I felt a pang of guilt that I'd not even sent in my re-application for grad school yet, as I'd promised them I would.

Parents. The arrival of Theresa Fiorino changed the picture somewhat. Clearly a take-charge kind of person, I could tell she would have El's every need attended to. Perhaps I wasn't required anymore. But even if it were true, El would be too kind to tell me so. Secretly, I thought El wanted me to stay and loved having me around. And I loved being around.

As I laid the last piece of silverware in its place setting, I made a decision. I would re-submit my grad school application online tonight, with a few tweaks highlighting my new skill set.

***

"Here's another donation to the silent auction," Spud called out then gave a fist pump into the air. I sighed and my gaze traveled from his jaunty beret to his mutton chops. If only he weren't such a coffee house hippy, because I really, really loved Spud's effervescent personality.

But mostly, I loved his kindness.

I went back to rearranging the already profuse selection of merchandise in the auction corner. "Darn! I don't think there's room for anything else. The party starts in two hours, and I'll have to make another bid sheet," I said as I hurried over to the bar. "What is it? Is it big?"

"Depends on your point of view," Spud said and winked at me before setting the manila envelope down on the counter in front of her. "It's a bit unusual but should draw a lot of interest."

My brow wrinkled in curiosity, noting the smug smile on Spud's face. I opened the envelope and read the contents. Unusual didn't begin to describe it. "Are you sure this is legal?"

Spud shrugged. "If it makes money, who cares?"

I read the letter again. A reserve bid of two hundred dollars for a date with Joe Thibault. "Who the heck is Joe Thibault?"

Spud lifted a shoulder and let it fall. "No idea, except it's one of the final two players for that pity roster spot on the Riot. According to the incredibly speedy Cole Fiorino, Joe's almost as fast. And a pretty good sport to help us out with the auction, I'd say. You know how many hockey groupies we get wandering in here because of Cole and Shred? They'll go bat-shit crazy for this guy. Hell, the bidding might go north of a grand." A diabolical clapping of hands accompanied Spud's gleeful comments, and I could almost see dollar signs in his eyes. But his enthusiasm was contagious and would only help the youth hockey program. Since I'd been there, I'd grown to care for the man like family. Like the brother I'd never had and always wanted. Darn and double darn.

After folding the letter back into its envelope, I gifted Spud my most charming smile. "Well, as long as it brings in money, who am I to argue?" Suddenly, my heart fluttered. Maybe this Joe guy would be the dream man I'd been waiting for – the one who'd walk into my life and sweep me off my feet just like Spud had said. Then I remembered he'd be a hockey player. *Curb the enthusiasm, Cinderella. No jock straps for you. Too much travel. And a huge ego on top of it.* I sighed my disappointment. "Who's the other finalist?"

Spud poured a beer on tap. "Name's Ryder Martin. Been in here quite a few times for lunch or dinner, so I'm sure you've seen him. He's a local – works for the Riot in corporate. According to Cole, he's pretty much a shoo in, so maybe I should say, used to work in corporate. Guess he's a regular ice monkey now."

"Oh." I shrugged. One hockey player was likely the same as another – witless and arrogant. Lots of brawn, not much brain. Good money gone bad. My sister's husband excluded, of course. But I had to admit, even though I adored Cole, and he was a great complement to my conservative sister, I wouldn't want to be married to him. "Good for him. So you know the guy pretty well then?" I'd never been to a game or even watched one on TV which I freely admitted, even to Cole. I was pucktarded.

Spud wiped the back of his hand across his forehead. "He's a good guy. Bit of a womanizer but then most of them are. I don't know anything about Thibault. Dude's Canadian."

Ha. I rest my case. I started toward the office to print off a new bid sheet, Ryder Martin completely forgotten, but stopped short as Eloise appeared in the doorway, clinging to the frame for support, her face pale as a ream of printer paper.

"Hannah," she said between gasps of air. "Call Cole, then call the hospital. I – I think I'm going into labor..." Her words were cut short as she grimaced in pain, her hand splayed across her belly.

"Oh my God," I shrieked, rushing toward her. "I knew it. I knew you'd be early. Because you're... you're... huge!" I took hold of El and guided her back to her office chair. "Sit down, don't move. I've got this." I dialed Cole's cell, and he answered on the first ring.

"Everything okay, babes?"

"I'm just fine," I replied, realizing I'd used El's phone again. "But you better get your wife to the hospital right now. Baby's coming early." He hung up without a reply. "He'll be right here," I said as I disconnected.

"Good," Eloise said, relief washing over her pale face. "The number for the hospital is on speed key three." I punched it. "Hanna-bee, I'm sorry, but looks like you'll need to manage things here tonight. Cole's depending on a successful fundraiser. Can you handle it?"

"But I want to be at the hospital with you," I said, heart falling to my feet. No. I didn't want to be in charge of some hockey-themed shindig. What if I made a fatal error because of my ignorance of the sport? "I promised Mom and Dad I'd look after you and Casa Fiorino, not the Rochester Riot."

Eloise bowed her head as she struggled through a contraction. I dropped to my knees beside her chair, not knowing how else to help my sister. No matter how many people were on hand, childbirth was one thing a woman had to do on her own.

"Obstetrics, Mayo Clinic," came a voice on the line. I gave Eloise's name and the name of her doctor. "We'll alert the attending physician. Bring her in as soon as you can."

Eloise relaxed as the contraction abated and took deep breaths. "Thanks, Hanna-bee. Just stay with me until Cole gets here. I'll have both him and my mother-in-law all over me. Two hot blooded Italians by my bedside will be all I can handle." She gave a weak smile. "You can help me best by taking charge here. Cole will be devastated if the fundraiser is a flop."

I nodded, then puffed up my chest in a show of confidence. I could do it. I would do it. "Okay. Don't worry about a thing."

Spud poked his head in the office. "Should I call an ambulance?" he asked, looking almost as pale as Eloise.

"No, Cole's on his way. Looks like it's you and me holding the fort tonight," I said.

He gave me a jaunty salute. "Roger that."

CHAPTER ELEVEN

Ryder

My nerves thrummed like live electrical wires as I neared the coach's office. This was it. The final cut. As promised, both players would receive a debriefing meeting with the coach, where we'd discuss our strengths and weaknesses, and how our skills did or did not fit the team. Whatever the commentary, only the outcome mattered to me. It meant everything. At this point, my last chance at my NHL dream, I didn't give a shit about improving on my well-known weaknesses. Steeling my spine, I knocked on the door.

"Come in." McTaggart rose from his desk as I entered. "Good morning, Ryder. How was your weekend?"

I shrugged, trying to basically forget the events of the last few days. "Just another few numbers on the calendar, that's all. Thanks for asking."

"Well, sit down. We have a few things to talk about." I sat and stared at the older man, trying to gauge the outcome before hearing the words. If this didn't go my way, I wanted to be able to mask my disappointment, so I didn't look like a whipped puppy when the abolishment of my hopes came crashing down around me like an imploded Las Vegas casino. "You nervous?"

"What gave you that impression," I said with a strained laugh.

"Oh, probably the sweat beads on your forehead. Relax. I've known you a long time. No need to be nervous."

Fucking A. Get on with it, man.

McTaggart returned to his seat opposite me, his expression annoyingly neutral. "Well, first of all, I want to thank you for all the time you've invested in the tryout process. This is a bit of an experiment for the league, and your professionalism is what makes it a success."

"It was my privilege," I said, fingers drumming on my knees. "I hope you liked what you saw."

"As I said, I've known you a long time, and the effort you displayed was beyond anything I've seen from you in the past. You're bigger, stronger, older yes, but still have passion for the game, and it shows. You wouldn't have made it this far if you didn't have what it takes."

"Thank you. I appreciate that." *Fuck, the suspense is killing me.* I shifted in my chair, heart pounding, palms sweating, ignoring the itch to wipe away the evidence of my distress on my suit pants.

"As you know, we have a pretty strong offensive unit, with guys like Fiorino and Jones on the roster. But new personalities can always inject new spark into a line, and an additional forward certainly wouldn't hurt the team."

Shit... is he seriously considering Tiny Thibault? My heart fell somewhere in the vicinity of my expensive Italian dress shoes. The same ones my old man had made fun of just that morning, calling me light in my fancy loafers.

"Similarly, the best scorers in the game need support at the other end. We need defenders, but what we really need is a two-way player, an offensive defenseman, if you will. Someone who can not only dig in the corners and protect the forward line, but also get on the scoreboard themselves with some regularity."

I found myself grinding my teeth again and forced my jaw to relax. "I understand."

Shane smiled as though amused at my stiffness. "I don't think you do. What I'm trying to say is..." he extended his hand across the desk, "welcome to the NHL."

All the air seemed to be sucked from the room as I tried to breathe in. My chest felt as though it would explode with the negative pressure. Was I hearing correctly? Was I still conscious?

"Well, don't just sit there, Martin. Do you accept or don't you?" McTaggart laughed, his hand dangling in the air. I reached for it in slow motion. My mind raced and pitched with thoughts of all the things I would say when this moment came, but suddenly I had no eloquent words, only one single syllable.

"Thanks."

***

"You going out?" my dad asked from his usual position in front of my big screen TV.

I pulled on my jacket and checked my tie in the mirror by the door. I'd feel more comfortable in jeans and a t-shirt, but I was representing the team now at a hockey function. Representing the team. *My* team. I still couldn't believe it and gave my tie such a fierce yank that I almost yelped in pain. *Yup, this shit is real.*

"Yeah. Don't wait up."

"Dressed pretty fancy for wherever you're going," my dad said, scanning my attire with disdain. "Hot date?"

I snorted a non-laugh. "This is how some people dress for work, actually. Not that you'd know."

"Most people don't work after five, smart ass," he scoffed. "I guess you come by it naturally though."

"I learned from the master." With the sharp verbal barb tangled in the tense air between us, I left my apartment and locked the door behind me. If only it were as easy to lock up my feelings behind that door along with my dying father.

Shit. Just like my mom. The pain of that loss had been buried long ago; it figured that my asshat father would be the one to dig it up again. And now there would probably never be the closure on the strained relationship that I so richly deserved after all that man had put me through over the years. But I couldn't imagine my proud and stubborn father ever admitting he might have gotten it wrong. Damn Braden and Colt. Why the fuck weren't they home dealing with this shit instead of leaving everything to me all the time?

Throwing off my morbid thoughts, I squared my broad shoulders, enjoying the feel of my renewed muscle mass straining beneath the material of my clothes. Fuck it. This was one night I would forget everything else and celebrate.

Ryder Martin, NHL star, has arrived.

On the drive to the restaurant, I went over the conversation again and again in my mind. Although I empathized with my dad over the man's terminal illness, I couldn't just erase over a decade of abuse and neglect. I sighed and ran a hand through my perfectly styled hair. The restaurant's outside lights loomed in the distance and I guided the luxury automobile smoothly into a parking space.

Damn it.

Even from outside I could see that Casa Fiorino was packed. Wall to wall bodies. My first team event and I'd be hankering to find the nearest escape route. I'd never been a fan of strangers brushing up against me at every angle. Unless those strangers were hot and loose females with wandering hands. No red carpet led to the door, but I guessed I could overlook that for the time being. I'd liked the place back when it was still the *Blues & Brews*, had tipped back many a beer within its walls.

But I hadn't been to the Casa since I'd first learned of the open tryouts for the Riot. Tonight, I saw it with new eyes and had to admit it looked much classier now since my rival – correction, teammate – had bought the place and turned it into an upscale Italian bistro.

A sandwich board in front of the entrance read, 'PRIVATE PARTY – ticket holders only.' I placed my hand on the latch and opened the door. The tantalizing smells of food and the pleasant rumble of happy crowd convo passed over me like a curtain, behind which I left all my concerns. Wrapping my tenuous confidence around me, I strode in through the entrance toward the hostess station where several people queued up to hand in their tickets. I'd made some calls and sold quite a few myself to help out Cole. With a stab of annoyance, I realized I'd forgotten the extras at home that could have been sold at the door.

Damn it. Ever since I'd been on cloud nine, I'd had my head up my own ass.

I moved forward as the bodies flowed into the main dining area. As I neared the hostess station, my jaw fell open an inch, and my eyes fluttered in surprise. And my cock. Well, that damn organ stirred to life for the first time in months, my balls tightening in my dress pants. Behind the small podium stood a gorgeous natural redhead wearing a sleeveless, pink satin dress with a sweetheart neckline that revealed just enough chest to be inviting rather than obvious. She must be new with the switchover. I knew Cole had kept on as many of Trey's employees as he could. And I'd have remembered seeing such a looker here before. Hell, I'd have flirted and tried to score with her for sure. Just my type with bangin' curves in all the right places and hair a man could get lost in.

Those long, auburn tresses glowed in the pin lights shining

down from overhead. I liked the way the ends brushed her bare shoulders as she moved. Fisting my hands to keep from reaching out, I longed to touch it, feel the silky length of it slide through my fingers before gliding my hand over that warm, creamy skin. I was betting the skin between her thighs would be just as warm. And moist. Ah, the pussy train was pulling into my station at last. This woman would be worth the pursuit.

"Ryder!" a voice called.

At the sound of my name, I turned to see Riot's winger, Ealon Jones, waving and edging his way toward me from inside. Jones grabbed me by the arm, pulling my attention away from the best view I could remember in a long time. "You don't have to stand in line, man. You're the main attraction tonight." He pulled me from the queue and into the hubbub of the main room. I cast a regretful backward glance at the hot girl, disappointed I didn't make it to the front of the line so I could talk to her. *Later, gorgeous girl.* But I'd already painted a mental bullseye right between her legs... er, eyes. "Hey, everybody!" Jones shouted. "Here's the man of the hour. No autographs, please."

I felt like I'd been pulled into the current of a river, except this one consisted of human bodies. A frisson of unease snaked up from my gut to tingle my spine. I wondered if I'd ever get used to being on display. Well, I'd have to learn to live with it. Being a professional athlete meant taking the good with the bad.

"Speak for yourself," I said amid a torrent of backslapping and hand shaking. I grinned so wide my cheeks began to hurt. We reached the bar, where a smiling Spud Davies greeted us. "What's your poison tonight, Ryder? On the house. Congrats, man!"

"Single malt on the rocks." I pointed a finger at Davies. "The good stuff, Spud. Don't hold out on me." Spud laughed and turned away to fetch the drink. I looked around. "Where's our esteemed proprietor? I don't see him."

"Oh, big news," Jones said. "Eloise went into labor this afternoon. The family's at the hospital. Cole's mom is in town. No word yet on a boy or girl. Even though Cole's been spouting male child ever since he found out El was pregnant, word on the street is that he doesn't know his ass from a hole in the ground."

"Really? That is big news." I tried hard to imagine the uptight, pencil-skirted, opinionated martinet who emasculated men like myself with her cock-shriveling words screaming her head off in a delivery room. Not a pretty picture but somehow gratifying after what she'd put me through. It would be a cold day in Hades before I'd need to beg for attention from the likes of tastee-freeze Eloise again. My mind drifted to Cole's flippant words about her sisters last time we'd cycled together. Seemed he really adored his new sisters-in-law, but I wondered if El's entire family dripped icicles from their limbs.

My scotch arrived, and I took that first smooth yet fiery sip. From now on, everything in my life would taste as sweet as this. Licking my lips, a grin split my face again. I was going to flirt my ass off tonight with every puck bunny in sight and end the months long drought. And get very, very drunk. All thoughts of my asshole father flying away on the wings of top shelf Glenfiddich.

CHAPTER TWELVE

Hannah

I turned my head at the sudden motion in the line, catching just a glimpse of a tall, hunky guy being pulled inside the restaurant. Though brief, what I could see of him caught my attention. His navy suit jacket stretched over his broad frame, his thick, sandy blond hair perfectly cut in a spiky style. The pearly grin on his face as his friend grabbed him flashed like a lighthouse beacon. His chiseled features reminded me of actor Ryan Reynolds. What a hottie. A spark of excitement sizzled up my spine as I mentally tallied the amount of tip money in my savings account. Would it be enough to buy Joe's date tonight if I wanted it?

What if that's him! It has to be!

"Miss?" the next person in line interrupted my thoughts.

"Hi," I said, snapping to attention. "Sorry. Ticket please?" I ripped the stub in half and deposited one end into a draw bowl. "Thanks so much for supporting Rochester youth hockey. Enjoy the party."

As the volume of patrons arriving at Casa Fiorino dwindled, I was anxious to close the doors and get inside to help out with the food and drinks. Truth be told, I was even more anxious for any news from the hospital. Obsessively, I checked my phone for what felt like the millionth time. A text from Cole said they were getting close and El was eight centimeters dilated. How long did it take to have one little baby? Especially one who seemed anxious to meet his or her parents enough to arrive ahead of schedule.

As I cleared the podium and prepared to seal the draw box, the entrance door swung open. An older man shuffled in, his clothes so rumpled and ill-fitting, he looked like something prior to the turn of the latest century. Not at all like the dresses and suits that filled the dining room at the moment. Perhaps he was lost and needed directions. "Hello, can I help you, sir?"

The man looked me up and down but not in a lascivious way – more curious than anything else. His gray hair thinned at the temples but was otherwise bushy and in need of a trim. "Uh, do I have the right address?" he croaked, his voice low and rough. He handed me a ticket from his jacket pocket.

I glanced at the stub. "You certainly do." The man seemed out of place, but my parents always told me to never judge a book by its cover. He could be some rich philanthropist in disguise for all I knew. Some people had a ton of money because they never spent any. I tore the ticket and gave the man his half.

"Thanks for your support. Please go right in."

Applause thundered in the dining room as I entered. The Riot's starting goalie Shredder Politski stood at the microphone, talking about the auction. I seemed to have missed the important player announcement while checking on the chicken sliders, clearing tables, and refilling the appetizer trays, my thoughts on my sister more than on the job.

"We have a very special item up for bid tonight," I heard Shredder say. "You may have seen this on television, but I'm pretty sure it's a first for Rochester. The next item on your auction list was graciously donated by one of our tryout participants, who sadly, did not make the final cut. But, since it's only fair that everyone gets a good look at what they're bidding on, c'mon up!" He curled his arm in a beckoning gesture.

I looked up as an athletic woman with long, copper-colored hair that cascaded down her back and shoulders in knotty curls stepped up beside the mic and waved to the crowd. Whistles and hoots sounded throughout the room. Her fresh, freckled face shone with good health, and her sleeveless sequined top revealed sculpted, shapely arms. Dewy pink lip gloss framed a stunning smile. She was gorgeous, really, especially with that thick mane of naturally wavy hair.

"Down boys," Shredder joked. "The bids will start at two-hundred, but I'm sure we can drive that number up. The winning bid will have the privilege of a date with this lovely young woman, who happens to be one hell of a hockey player. We called her Joe, but it's my pleasure to introduce, hailing from La Ronge Saskatchewan, Miss Josée Marie Thibault!"

At Shredder's announcement, my mouth dropped open. My dream man was a woman! They allowed women in the NHL? I'd had absolutely no idea. As I gaped at the scene feeling beyond stupid, my cell phone buzzed in my pocket. Grabbing it and clutching it tight, I moved to a quieter corner. "Hello?"

"It's a girl," Cole's voice crackled over the connection. He sounded exhausted and delirious. "Five pounds, six ounces. She's beautiful! Just like her mother."

I smiled at the news, my heart squeezing in my chest. A niece! I could already imagine spoiling her rotten with frilly outfits and everything pink. "Of course she is! What's her name? How's El?"

"El's fine, no name yet, she's..." his voice cracked and stalled.

My heart whomped against my ribs. "What? Is anything wrong?"

"No, it's just... she's just so small, she'll have to stay in the hospital for a while."

"Yes, I suppose that's what they do," I said, not having the first clue how premature babies were handled. "But it's the best hospital in the country, right? Everything's going to be fine."

"Is that the wise old auntie talking?" Cole chuckled.

Auntie. Holy crap, I'm an auntie! "That's right. So you just listen to me, Daddy-o." Even through the noise all around me, I could hear it. The big tough hockey guy was about to cry.

"Daddy-O..." he repeated in a choked voice, followed by silence. "Hannah, I can't even explain how I'm feeling right now. I never thought I was capable of loving someone this much. Like all the love in the whole world isn't enough to explain how full my heart is. In the blink of an eye."

Tears pricked the backs of my eyelids too. I took a deep breath and changed the subject to ease the moment. "Well, things are going great here, don't worry about anything. Spud and I and your teammates have got everything under control."

Cole cleared his throat. "Right. That's great, I knew you could handle it. Kick-start that party with some champagne, will you? Tell Spud to break out the bubbly, on the house. Everyone in my Casa needs to raise a glass of the finest to baby girl Fiorino!"

"Okay," I said. "Right after I call Mom, Dad, and Sophia in Columbus."

"Already done. My mother's called everyone we're related to on two continents. We're gonna have one hell of a cell bill. I better go stop her before she gets on the horn to NBC."

A joyous giggle escaped my lips. "Alright then, I'll be at the hospital first thing in the morning. Give El a kiss for me, and your new daughter too. I expect to hear a name when I get there, okay?"

"Okay, Auntie Hannah."

Auntie Hannah. I liked the sound of that. After I disconnected the call, I weaved my way through the jostling bodies to tell Spud the news. His mutton-chop jaw lit up with a big grin. "Go tell Shredder to make an announcement while I start pouring."

CHAPTER THIRTEEN

Ryder

"You're fucking kidding me," I said, staring at the copper haired stunner standing next to Shredder. Had I known this information prior to the open call, I might have opted to forgo my dream in favor of my eviscerated pride. "I had to beat out a chick? That's disgraceful. That's... embarrassing." I turned to Jones, whose gaze was fixed blankly ahead. I elbowed him. "That's the worst fucking thing I've ever heard in my life."

"What?" Jones said, clearly oblivious to everything except the girl at the microphone.

I threw my hands up in the air. "A chick, *he's* a chick! How did we not know this? Is this Sheehan Murphy's kind of warped version of PUNKd? That old coot would do just about anything to make a buck, but shitting all over the NHL and making a mockery of our sport? It's... it's..."

Jones just stared, his eyes as glassy as if he'd imbibed an entire bottle of scotch. "It's I dunno, bro. All I know is that holy fuck, she's hot. Too bad she never showered with me. I could have soaped her up good."

I raked a shaky hand through my hair. "I can't believe it. All these weeks we were skating, sweating, spitting, and swearing right next to that juicy number. If I didn't hate her guts, I'd buy the date just so I could sweat and spit all over her. How the hell did she keep that shit hidden?"

"Definitely bidding on that piece of ass," Ealon said, knocking back another tequila shot. "Time to teach her a lesson about infiltrating a man-only situation. Fuck. Is nothing sacred anymore? Pretty soon we'll have chicks on the bus and chicks on the plane and chicks..."

"Someone will outbid you," I said. "You're notoriously cheap. If you heard the gossip in the front office, you wouldn't be so cocky. You should take it easy on those," I pointed to Ealon's empty shot glass, "you know what they say about tequila... it never travels alone."

"Look who's talking. If you're counting, I believe that's your third scotch. No game 'til Monday, bro. You gotta learn to live like a player now." Jones slammed the tiny tumbler down on the bar and straightened. "Time to put my money where my mouth wants to be... in between those freckled thighs." He laughed and headed for the auction tables. "I hope she doesn't smell like one of my teammates, like Fiorino."

I waved my glass at Spud. "Another," I said, my words drowned by the pop of a cork. It reminded me of what Jones's cock was probably doing right about now. "Aw, you didn't have to break out the Moet & Chandon just for me." Spud wobbled and I saw two of him. The scotch was definitely kicking in. Damn straight.

Spud poured the foaming liquid into waiting glasses lined up on a tray. "Seems you're not the only thing we're celebrating tonight."

"Huh?"

"Attention, everyone," Shredder's voice boomed from the front of the room. "I have some great news. I've just been informed that we have another addition to the team. It's a bit earlier than expected, but the Fiorino family has just increased by one. Tonight, Cole and Eloise are the proud parents of a baby girl."

Shouts and cheers filled the room. I whistled and shook my

foggy head. "That stupid ass," I mumbled. "Just because you repeatedly say the word boy, doesn't make it so. What do you know? Fiorino the Great will be stickhandling diapers instead of pucks. Hope he remembers which bag to grab on game nights."

Spud laughed at my comment and slid a glass of champagne across the bar at me. "Here. This'll hold you until I bring you that scotch."

"Gee, thanks. Just what I wanted... fruit punch." I took the glass anyway and raised it in a small salute. As I turned around, my body connected with something solid, followed by the sound of tinkling glass. "Shit," I yelled, grabbing for the serving tray I'd just knocked out of a woman's hands, dropping my own glass to land on the toe of my polished shoe.

Champagne flew everywhere, spewing onto the floor, onto the sleeves of my new team jersey, and the pink satin material of her dress. Christ, I was drunker than I thought. "Sor..." I started to say, when I looked up into the widest, bluest eyes I'd ever seen. And they looked like they wanted to kill me as daggers blazed from their azure depths. If I weren't so numb from scotch, I'd feel them pepper my face. Frozen in their icy glare, I said the first thing that popped into my blurry brain. "Sorry, miss."

Their owner stood as still as me, liquid dripping from her chin and forming little rivers down the skin of her neck and chest. I watched a droplet roll down and disappear in the cleft between her breasts. Her lips trembled as she found her voice. *No. No. No. Please don't cry.* "You should be."

Of all the ways I'd have wanted to bump into the pretty redhead from the front entrance, this was not it. "I really am. I am so, so sorry."

In a flash, Spud appeared at my elbow, prying loose the oval tray from my fingers. "I've got this," he said, thoughtfully producing a towel for the lady. "Sit down, Ryder, before you fall down." He swept up the scattered champagne glasses from the floor and carried them away.

"*You're* Ryder Martin? The new player?" she asked, clutching the towel in her hands. She seemed to have found her composure. And her angry voice.

I smiled weakly. "Yeah. How do you like me so far?"

She dabbed the drops off her chin and then threw the towel in my face. I fell back onto my barstool as though the weight of the cloth had pushed me there. Pulling it off, I stared after her as she marched away, the folds of her pink skirt swishing between her lovely legs. She disappeared into the kitchen without a backward glance.

"Aw, fuck," I grumbled, tossing the towel onto the bar. *Off the post and out.* "Where's my fucking drink? I really need it after that shitshow."

I twisted around to find that Spud had also exited. Pushing myself to my feet, I went in search of Jones. I found him chatting up 'Tiny' Thibault in a corner. Damn, she had a nice figure. Especially when poured into that tight-fitting sequined number that barely covered her ass. She turned toward me as I approached.

"Allo Ryder," she said in a telltale French accent, flashing me a smile along with a copious expanse of fleshy leg. My eyes couldn't help but travel the length of it. "Congratulation... de best man win, after all." She reached out for a handshake.

Very punny. I swayed on my feet, my hand feeling as if it were caught in a vice. *Strong too.* "Thanks. Is this left-handed cherry picker bothering you, Joe?"

Ealon threw me a caustic look, then leaned in and sniffed me. "You're supposed to drink the champagne not take a bath in it, dipshit. I'm not sure I'm going to be okay with you on the team. Am I going to have to explain everything?"

"Oh, he is celebrating, Ealon. Let him enjoy it," Josée said, waving off my appearance with a very feminine giggle. I castigated myself again for not seeing what was right underneath my nose the entire time. How in the hell could I have missed it?

"I like a girl who's a good sport," I said with a wink. "Sorry you didn't make the team, but I'm sure we could play with each other again sometime."

Josée smiled despite my lame come-on and glanced over my shoulder. "I think someone wants to meet you." A giggle sounded from behind. I turned, slowly this time.

Two girls stood shoulder to shoulder, their eyes bright with a champagne-induced sparkle. *And fake ID's most likely.* Neither looked of legal drinking age to me, but what the hell. They were here. And they were looking at me – no, drooling over me more like.

"Can we have your autograph?" The one on the right squeaked, her dark bangs brushing just above her over-manicured eyebrows.

"Me too?" the other mewed, her waist-length hair tamed behind a wide hairband.

"Certainly, ladies..." I acknowledged coolly. "You have a pen?" Bangs-girl smiled and produced a Sharpie but nothing else. I took it and gave her a curious look. "Uh, what do you want me to sign?"

The pair looked at each other, laughed and returned their attention to him. On cue, they pulled aside the necklines of their flimsy dresses and pointed to the area of skin just above their hearts.

"Us!"

After signing their naked skin, I capped their Sharpie and sent them on their way only to have a new pair take their place. It seemed a line was forming.

"Oh shit, looks like we've got an ambulance case on our hands," Jones mumbled over the lip of his beer bottle.

It registered that Ealon had said something, but I was too busy posing for selfies with an unending stream of girls that I didn't quite catch it. Jesus, they circled like seagulls over a fishing dock at high tide. But after my interlude with the lady in pink, none of them were floating my boat even though they were literally throwing their naked tits in my face.

"Say what?" I called over.

Jones took another swig then pointed the neck of the bottle toward the bar. "Code red. No country for old men." Out of curiosity, I threw a casual glance in that direction, but then did a double take. My vision might not be the most reliable after all the drinks, but what I saw nearly made me fall down. How the fuck did that piece of work get in here since he didn't have a pot to piss in, let alone funds for a high-ticket fundraiser?

I could only stare as I watched my bent, miserable old man being lifted out of his chair and escorted off the premises – by none other than the miss pretty in pink. The only woman my cock wanted and whose acquaintance I'd screwed up royally. Apparently, my father had more charm than I did.

"Who is that old reprobate?" Jones asked. "How the hell did he get in here?"

I felt a burning sensation at the base of my tongue, a precursor to a potential vomit-storm, but I choked it back. "No idea," I lied through clenched teeth.

CHAPTER FOURTEEN

Hannah

As if the evening wasn't stressful enough already, I had to end up all wet.

I stood before the bathroom mirrors, assessing the damage. The torrent of spilled liquid left blotchy patches in my makeup and a big wet stain on the front of my dress. Hot tears threatened to melt off my mascara too. I'd spent hours altering the bridesmaid gown I'd worn at Sophia's wedding into a short cocktail dress especially for this occasion. Since it had sentimental value, I prayed it would come clean.

The worst part was standing nose to nose with the man who'd ruined it. On top of the mysterious Joe Thibault turning out to be a woman, the gorgeous Ryan Reynolds lookalike I'd seen jumping the queue at the entrance turned out to be not only the Riot's newest player and the guest of honor but also a drunken klutz. And a womanizing piece of shit if Spud's words rang true. And Spud was a man who could be depended on. He never lied. And Ryder's first impression of me would be looking like a drowned rat and glaring daggers of outrage at him.

Hardly love at first sight.

Ugh. Why couldn't I meet somebody I was actually attracted to in a normal way? Like at a bookstore perusing the gourmet cooking section or a coffee shop where he'd stoop chivalrously to pick up my dropped change? Or over powdered sugar donuts at the convenience store like Cole and El. Why did it have to be so hard?

However, the disastrous encounter didn't make Ryder Martin any less handsome. In that blistering moment when his soft, amber-brown eyes had locked with mine, I'd felt like a trapped animal, desperate to run away yet frozen in the hypnotizing gaze of my hunter. But the spell had broken along with the shattered glassware all around us.

He's not for the likes of you, Hanna-bee. This was one situation where my other alter-ego Wanna-bee made more sense. I wasn't enough to capture the attention of a man like that. So it was good that I didn't want his attention.

I really didn't want it.

After I heaved a sigh, I wondered if I'd ever convince myself of that. If I could just get this night over with, I could go to the hospital and see Eloise and the baby – a place I'd much rather be right now. But I'd made a promise. To conceal my ruined frock, I donned a black cardigan that El kept on the back of her office chair and marched back to the battlefield looking like an advertisement for Nike compression pants.

I picked up another tray of filled champagne glasses from the bar, thankfully noting Ryder had left his previous roost and gone elsewhere. I moved carefully around the room, and as I passed the auction tables saw something I immediately wished I hadn't. Ryder stood there, surrounded by women. He leaned over one of them, his hands on her huge boobs. What in the hell was he doing? Inappropriate much? Geez, give a guy a shot at the NHL and he turns into some kind of exhibitionist.

As I stepped closer, I saw a pen in his hand. Good heavens, was he *writing* on the girl's exposed cleavage? Something coiled up my spine like a poisonous serpent, bitter and feral. I froze in place, unable to move or look away, watching him appear to take great delight inscribing atop the skin of her left breast. In the same moment, as though he sensed my presence or the heat of my glare, he glanced up. The expression 'like a deer in headlights' must have originated in Minnesota, because even from several feet away, I saw the whites enlarge around his beautiful brown irises.

Suddenly, my paralysis released, and I spun an about-face, feeling... what? Disgust? Embarrassment? Jealousy? *Ridiculous.* The guy was clearly an ass, a skirt-chasing ice monkey with loose hands and even looser morals. I wanted nothing to do with that sort, hot looks or not. The saying was true. You really couldn't judge a book by its cover. Even when that cover had big broad shoulders and dreamy brown eyes. And some kind of hypnotic and magnetic pull that drew me toward him like a hiker to the edge of a cliff.

I shook my head to eradicate any further images of him and continued serving the last glasses of bubbly in honor of my precious new niece, trying to erase the image from my mind. But like a bad celebrity out-take in a gossip rag, once you saw it, you couldn't un-see it.

On my way back to the kitchen for more glassware, I noticed the gray-haired man who'd ambled in at the last minute sitting alone in a corner next to a wall. He hunched awkwardly over the bar top. It made me sad to see his isolation, but even more worried. Was he alright? Had he had too much to drink, or something worse – a seizure of some sort? My stomach lurched. I didn't know if anyone working tonight even had first-aid training. The last thing this night needed to cap it off was a visit from an EMT, sirens blaring and strobes flashing.

"Sir?" I asked. "Can I help you? Get you anything?" As I drew near, I saw his shoulders moving up and down as his lungs worked to take in air. His breathing sounded labored and painful, rasping in and out. He raised his head at the sound of my voice, placed a shaking hand flat on the bar to push himself upright.

"Just... catching my breath," he gasped, his voice tight and harsh. "Be... okay." His movement revealed the half full whiskey glass he'd been guarding beneath his chest.

My worried eyes scanned his slight frame. "Do you want to go home? I can call a taxi for you."

He nodded haltingly. "Yes. I gotta... get outta here." At close range, I noticed his pockmarked face and reddened nose. He smelled strongly of liquor.

"Okay, just take it easy and stay right here. I'll call one right now." I reached for my cell phone and called the local cab company the restaurant utilized as I hurried over to where Spud stood pulling pints from the taps. "There's a gentleman over there who's not doing too well. I'm calling him a cab."

Spud looked over. "Good. Can you handle it? Got my hands full here."

"Sure. He's not causing any trouble." When the taxi arrived, I went to the elderly man and slipped a hand under his elbow. "Taxi's outside, sir. Let me help you."

The man seemed a bit recovered but still shaken. "Thanks." He attempted a smile as he allowed me to guide him off his seat and to the door. "What's a nice girl like you doing escorting broken-down has-beens like me out of bars? You're beautiful and sweet like an angel. You could do better. You could be anything you wanted to be."

I chuckled at the words I'd always wanted to hear from my own father but was still waiting for. I wouldn't hold my breath since I perpetually lived in El's shadow. "Just lucky I guess, but I sure appreciate your kind words. You take care of yourself, okay? Thank you for coming and supporting youth hockey. Goodnight."

On a whim, I leaned over and kissed him on the cheek. His

look of abject pleasure stole my breath. Did this man not have anyone to care about him? He nodded as the driver assisted him into the back seat. As the car drove away, I waved until he was out of sight and I thought of my dad again. *A grandpa,* I reminded myself, a twinkle of excitement returning at the news of El's new daughter. He was probably handing out cigars at the union hall right now. The firstborn of his firstborn.

I guess we were lucky to have a dad with plenty of years left to enjoy with his grandkids and not in the kind of condition as the man I'd just sent home in a cab.

Sucking in a deep breath, I went back inside. Life in Rochester was turning out to be quite an education. At this rate, I might not even need grad school.

***

"Christina Theresa Fiorino," I repeated as I peered through the glass of the incubator unit. An awfully big name for such a little person. Barely the length of my forearm, baby Christina sported an unlikely shock of black hair on her tiny head which was, no doubt, the legacy of both her parents' luxurious tresses. I stared in awe at the little wonder of nature, her face with its translucent infant's skin relaxed in oblivious slumber, breathing on her own despite the numerous sensors and tubes connected to her small body. Now I knew why cherubs were always depicted the way they were. Babies were the closest thing to angels that Earth possessed.

"Well, what do you think, Auntie Hannah?"

I turned to see Eloise standing close behind me. "No more Hanna-bee?" I said with a grin.

El shook her head. "No way. You're officially an adult when you reach aunt status."

I wrapped my sister in a gentle hug. "Thank goodness. She's

so beautiful, El. I can hardly believe she's real. When can I hold her?"

"She should be ready to go home in a week or two. When the doc gives the thumbs up, you'll be first in line."

"After Mom and Dad, I assume. Are they going to come out early? Have you talked to them?"

"I've sent pictures, but Dad can't get away until the twenty-third. We'll all be home and ready for Christmas visitors by then. So?" She nudged my elbow. "How'd the party go? How much money did we raise? Was the place full?"

I laughed at my big sis. "Jeez, El, can't you relax and enjoy motherhood for five minutes? Does it always have to be business for you?"

"Sorry. Old habits die hard, I guess," she said with a sigh. El looked tired. Still beautiful but like she'd been through the ringer. Thank goodness my own childbirth was still years in the future. "Tell me anyway."

I rolled my eyes heavenward, exasperated. "Spud has the totals. I was so tired after the cleanup, I just went home." I sighed thinking about all the crazy things that happened. "It certainly was a night to remember." *Or one to forget.*

"Did you meet anyone interesting?" El prodded. "I'm sure most of the team was in attendance."

I wrinkled my nose as if something or *someone* stunk and shook my head. "I was too busy to notice."

El cocked her head and narrowed her eyes in suspicion. "Hannah Jane Robertson, you are a terrible liar. Too busy to notice a herd of hunky men all around you?" She clucked her tongue. "What did you think of Shredder? He and Cole are old friends from way back, and he married my favorite assistant and friend, Kylie." She leaned over and lowered her voice. "He's my favorite Riot player next to my husband. And even if you didn't notice anyone, I'm willing to bet at least one of them noticed you."

Yeah. One of them sure did. And not in a good way.

I shrugged. "I loved Shredder. He did a great job hosting the event, and I think his charm and sense of humor drew more money in. And as for the Riot players noticing me? Doesn't matter. I've re-submitted my grad school application. I'll be going back to Columbus eventually anyway."

El nodded. "Really? That's great. If that's what you want. You know, there's some pretty good schools out here too. Minnesota boasts some of the top private colleges in the country."

My lips pressed together in a tight line. "Yes. Especially the Rochester school of hard knocks. It's teaching me life skills I won't soon forget."

Like whenever you see a man that makes your heart pound and your panties wet... run.

CHAPTER FIFTEEN

Ryder

All I could see through the slits of my puffy eyelids was a furry face with glassy eyeballs staring back at me. I jerked my head back on reflex, my brain responding with an explosion of pain that reached to every part of my skull, including my hair follicles. A pitiful groan escaped from my dry lips.

With difficulty, I pushed up off my pillow, blinking to clear what felt like radioactive waste coating my eyes. My bed companion lay unblinking on the pillow next to me – a small stuffed toy that looked like it came from Build-A-Bear. It wore a plastic hockey helmet on its head and fuzzy felt skates on its feet. Emblazoned on its little jersey in black marker were the words, 'I LUV U RYDER.' The stuffed toy was probably the best-looking thing I'd had in my bed in recent months.

What. The. Fuck.

I glanced around my bedroom for any other surprise inhabitants and thankfully found none. Alone, whew. I honestly didn't remember how I got home. Flopping onto my back, I raised my arm to cover my eyes that now throbbed like nuclear reactor cores. As I crooked my elbow, I saw curvy writing on my inner forearm in a matching black ink. CHELSI, with a heart dotting the 'I' and a phone number. I groaned again and clamped my aching orbs shut.

Be careful what you wish for, I chided myself. Regret and worry crept into my brain in equal doses. Had this Chelsi been here and left? Did we get it on? Was she the brunette-bangs-girl or her friend? Or someone else entirely? Fuck me, I couldn't remember at all.

None of it past the point where Jones had called out my dying old man as a reprobate which had put me straight up over the edge and further into my cups.

As the memories flooded back, I imagined with horror, the sight of my dad lurking in the shadows of the bar. Spying on me? Following me? More likely following the scent of a free drink. He must have found the unsold tickets lying around and decided they were a gift. How long was he there, and how much did he see or hear? Probably enough to know about my selection to the team. Unless he was already so deep into the pail he'd fallen both deaf and blind.

I bolted upright, ignoring my splitting head. Where was the old man? *Shit.* The man was sick to begin with, and my last glimpse of him involved his removal from the restaurant by...

My mental movie went to freeze-frame. That girl. That lovely auburn-haired nymph I'd wanted to meet all night... until I'd doused my chances at the same moment I'd doused her with spilled champagne.

Well, that vision was lost to me forever.

I stumbled out of my room to check on my dad, grabbing my bathrobe on the way. The Murphy bed in my den hadn't been turned down, and there was no sign of the man anywhere. Panic, guilt, and nausea collapsed upon me all at once. As much as I hated him, I still felt responsible. I hadn't pictured my Saturday starting out with calls to every hospital in Rochester.

By mid-afternoon, I'd located him at the Mayo Clinic's Pulmonary Care center. He told me that he'd taken a cab straight there from the restaurant and that they'd kept him overnight.

After some juice and a quick shower, I drove to Mayo and

found my father's room. He lay still in the bed, hooked up to monitors that beeped quietly through the room in the clinic's observation ward for pulmonary patients.

I stared with tired eyes at my father. "Do you even have any insurance coverage?" I asked him. "Or are you expecting me to foot the bill for all this." I circled my finger around the room. My guilt didn't quite extend as far as paying thousands of dollars in unexpected medical bills.

Dad coughed again, as he'd been doing every few minutes since I arrived. He seemed worse than when I'd picked him up two weeks ago.

"The FMC arranged for an outpatient program with Mayo before I got released," he said when his lungs settled down enough to speak. "They want research subjects for my condition. They're working on nearby co-op accommodations for patients so they can study the disease."

I stared at my father. "Why the hell didn't you tell me this before?"

"You never asked. And why the hell didn't you tell me about an NHL contract? Thought for sure you'd wanna rub that in my face the first chance you got instead of keeping it a secret." His bloodshot eyes narrowed. "Don't worry about denting that fat wallet of yours, whelp. The research department pays part of it, and I still have a pension. So I'll stay here until then."

I took a step closer. "You wouldn't be here at all if you hadn't helped yourself to those charity tickets. The free drinks were on Cole Fiorino and only for the paying customers making a donation. Just couldn't wait to hit the sauce again, could you?"

He seemed to shrink and collapse into the thin mattress of his bed at this comment, as though he'd aged another ten years in the minutes we'd spent arguing. Emotions warred within me and my own chest felt tight with anger, frustration, anguish.

Mostly helplessness. I shouldn't have said that. Words couldn't hurt my father more than he hurt already. All of a sudden, being right didn't seem that important. I'd just realized my own dream, and I could afford to be more empathetic as I tried to forget all the pain this man had caused to my family and forge some peace before...

"Son," he wheezed. "I'm sorry for intruding on your important evening. I'm sorry for a lot of things. Your mother. The accident. I'm sorry I won't get to see your brothers before I leave this world. But more than anything, I'm sorry I won't get to see you live your dream." He lifted a trembling hand. "Go away. I need some time to myself."

***

It took several hours and about a gallon of black coffee before I recovered from my emotional exchange with my father, and my hangover reduced to a low-grade case of indigestion. Add that to piecing together the events of the previous evening, and I realized I owed some apologies. Lots of them. Some even to myself. I'd behaved like an entitled, spoiled, first-class asshat. But one, in particular, I wanted to deliver in person and say out loud.

With my tail between my legs, I found myself on the steps of Casa Fiorino, wondering what sort of reaction might await me inside its doors. Maybe she wouldn't even be inside. I had no idea about her schedule. Hell, I didn't even know her name. But I couldn't get the girl out of my mind. Even if she hadn't been stunningly attractive, she still stood out among the throng of women in the place last night. She shone like a lighthouse beacon across a rolling sea of party girls and hockey wife wanna-bees. Those chicks that would do anything to bag a professional athlete and suck him dry just to say they had. The lady in pink... seemed so different. So unaffected by the presence of professional athletes. So sweet. And innocent.

I let out an ironic chuckle. My infantile ranking scale of female candidates centered around the four Fs – fitness, fertility, flexibility, and fuckworthiness. I hadn't thought of sweetness or innocence being qualities I'd ever want in a woman, but perhaps that was why she fascinated me. One always wanted what they'd never had. And I wouldn't forget her steady, caring nature. In addition to putting up with my own and others drunken foolery, she'd helped an old codger she didn't know from Adam in his time of need. Acts like that required fortitude and a kind heart.

I slapped a shaky hand to my head, wondering what the hell my father might have divulged to the woman. Any words tumbling from the old man's lips couldn't paint me in a favorable way. In the cold light of day, I felt ashamed for not getting involved and going to my dad's aid. It was even worse since our conversation earlier today.

What kind of shit son are you? The archetypal angel on one shoulder whispered in my ear. *Same kind of shit father he was to you,* replied the little red devil.

But I'd been pretty drunk myself by that time and not thinking clearly or rationally. The shock of seeing my old man in the place, uninvited on top of my compromised state, had paralyzed me, keeping my mouth shut. I didn't want anyone knowing the relationship between us. Especially not her.

Christ, I didn't even know her name yet. But I'd never find out if I didn't walk through that door, so I pulled the latch and stepped over the threshold. The dinner rush hadn't yet begun, so the place was quiet. With my heart squeezing in my chest, I spotted her auburn head in the middle of the dining room where she leaned over a table setting wine glasses in place. I sipped in a breath and ventured farther into the room.

"Excuse me." With a start at my voice, she turned toward me, hair swirling in a glossy arc about her shoulders as she did so. *Shit, she's something.* Her expression was difficult to define. One of recognition but neither hostile nor welcoming. "Hi, there."

"Hello," she replied with a nod.

Mouth suddenly dry, I asked, "Remember me?"

Is that the best thing you can come up with, dipshit?

Her lips pursed into an alluring pucker as she regarded me. I hovered by the hostess stand, not knowing if I could get any closer. Or if I should even try. Her full lips looked pink and petal-soft, and right then and there I wanted to kiss her. To tell her with my body what my bumbling words could never do. Kiss away whatever sourness I'd placed there with my careless behavior from the night before.

Her eyes seemed to pepper me with tiny ice picks. "Hard to forget. You were the guest of honor, after all."

I scrubbed a hand down my face. "Yeah, I guess. Well, I came to apologize."

She gave a small shrug. "It's okay. Don't worry about it. Accidents happen in restaurants all the time. I've gotten worse things than expensive champagne spilled on me before."

I shook my head and felt as if I could walk a few steps toward her. "It's not okay. I'm normally much less clumsy and much less drunk. I gave you a rough time, and I want to make it up to you."

Her eyes narrowed, and I thought I saw a flash of pain sweep across her beautiful features. My heart sank again knowing I'd put it there by being a jackass.

She tugged her full lower lip between her teeth. "That dress was my bridesmaid's dress from my sister's wedding. You can't make up for something like that. It's silk. Not even dry-cleaning can save it."

I straightened my back and shoved my hands in my jacket pockets. This wasn't going so well. I took another step closer. "Okay. I really am sorry about that. Look, can we start over? I'm Ryder. What's your name?"

She seemed to think about it for a minute, as though deciding if I was worth trusting with even that small bit of information. "Hannah," she finally said, still not releasing her rigid posture. Her stiff stance told me more than words. I wasn't welcome and that knowledge stung more than anything.

"Hello, Hannah. Pleased to meet you. Will you accept my apology and allow me to save at least some face by taking you out to dinner? I won't be able to sleep at night until I make some kind of reparation to you."

She glanced left and right. "Uh, I work in a restaurant, in case you haven't noticed."

Gah, I couldn't catch a break with this woman. "Right, how about a hockey game? It's my first game with the Riot this week, and I'm kinda nervous. Would be nice to have a friend in the stands."

"A friend? You seemed to have lots of friends last night," she said, sarcasm lacing her voice. "And I don't really follow hockey. I've never been to a game. Despite working here, it's not my favorite sport."

Ouch. Two shots. Both of them blocked. Yeah, I'd gotten a little carried away last night and was rather embarrassed at all the attention I'd received from all the bare-chested groupies. But man, I hadn't had to work so hard in a conversation since my date with Eloise. How could this girl live in Rochester, work in a joint owned by a pro hockey player, located only a few blocks from the arena, and not be interested in hockey? In

Minnesota. The fucking *state* of hockey.

I lifted my hands from my pockets and spread them wide. "Well, there's a first time for everything. Give it a try? You just might like it."

A trace of a smile began to bloom on her delicate face. At last, the storm clouds were breaking, allowing a little light to peek through. To me, it was more than a smile – it was the sunrise of a new day. One where I hadn't made any mistakes yet, and I hoped to keep it that way. I held my breath on a prayer as I awaited my fate.

"Alright," she said. "Spud keeps telling me I should get out more. I'm new to the city, and I haven't seen much of it since I've been so busy working."

I smiled back. "Well, you came at the right time. Rochester is at its best in winter. You'll love it once you get to know it."

She looked at me curiously. "How do you get to know a place when it's so cold out?"

"By embracing it," I said. "When are you off work? If you're not up for a professional game, I could show you around, give you some winter survival tips."

"I-I'm on the late shift today," she said, her smile fading.

No, no, no. Don't let that sun go down.

"Tomorrow then. You must be off on a Sunday, right? Around two o'clock? I'll pick you up. Where do you live?"

***

Déjà vu passed over me like a rippling curtain as I pulled up in front of the address Hannah had given me. Wasn't this the same building where I'd dropped off Eloise after our date so long ago? I brushed off the memory like a piece of lint. I didn't know where Mr. and Mrs. Fiorino made their home now. Some fancy suburb, most likely. Didn't matter. All my senses now focused on the girl walking down the steps from the entrance. I jumped out from behind the wheel of my Lexus to open the passenger door.

With the temperature inching toward zero, she looked dressed for the weather, wearing fleece leggings and tall boots. Her hip-length belted jacket had fur trim on the sleeves and collar, and her hair fell in silky ribbons from beneath a cute knitted Sherpa cap with pompoms dangling from the ears. She looked as fresh and bright as the crisp December day around us and lust hit me square in the gut.

"Hi," I said, brushing it away. I'd vowed to be on my best behavior. "You look great, Hannah. Ready for the great white north?"

She smiled, an authentic one this time, that dimpled her cheeks and illuminated her large blue eyes. Cornflowers, that was it. The color of cornflower blossoms. I'd never look at that particular bloom the same way again.

"Thank you," she replied, holding her arms out to the sides. "Well, you said to embrace it... so I thought I should be insulated."

How about I embrace you, gorgeous... keep you warmer than that coat ever could. I inhaled the chilly air to cool off my baser thoughts as I helped her into the warm luxury of my car. I wanted to impress her, not club her over the head like a caveman. *As tempting as that thought is.*

"So where are we going?" she asked brightly, her petal-pink lips stretching across the curve of her brilliant white smile. She reminded me of a piece of glossy ribbon candy – the kind you know you shouldn't eat but are eventually going to give in to. A lollipop in rainbow colors. And I wanted to lick it. Instead, I put a hand on the gear shift and slipped it into drive.

"I've got some ideas," I said with a smug grin.

She laughed out loud, the sound even sweeter than a ringer off the post and in. "That's Buddy the Elf talking. I've seen that movie. Let me guess, first stop is a crappy cup of coffee?"

"Followed by a spin in the revolving door at Macy's," I said, picking up on the joke. "Actually I thought I'd save the coffee for last, to warm us up for afters."

"Okay," she said, nodding. "Sounds practical."

Practical was the last adjective I wanted applied to a date with me, but I had a sense that 'ahead slow' would be the road sign for today's journey. Something I wasn't used to, but definitely fell into the 'low risk, high reward' category I favored. Dipping into Hannah's sweet rewards would be worth the leisurely stroll. Glancing at those full lips I coveted, I wondered if I'd get an opportunity to steal a kiss from them before the date ended.

I hoped an appropriate moment would present itself because I couldn't remember being attracted to a woman so much.

First, I decided on a circle tour of central Rochester. Frost-encrusted trees lined the boulevards, and light drifts of snow gathered against curbs and fences along the way. We started near the Mayo Civic Center, driving south by the Apache Mall and Soldier's Field, then northwest past Cascade Lake Park. Finally, we cut eastward to connect with North Broadway, crossed the river, and pulled into the parking lot at the Rochester Recreation Centre. The packed snow crunched beneath the car's wheels as I came to a stop.

"All right, now you've seen the highlights from the safety of the bus, time for the group activity portion of the tour," I announced.

Hannah looked at me from beneath the brim of her pompom covered hat. "Like?"

I wiggled my eyebrows up and down, villain-style. "What

size boots do you wear?"

"For what?" she asked warily.

"Something I'm actually fairly coordinated at, unlike navigating crowded rooms. Skating."

Her impossibly blue eyes went wide. "I don't know how to skate."

"Well, you're in luck because you've got a coach right here," I said, gesturing to myself. "C'mon. They have rentals inside."

CHAPTER SIXTEEN

Hannah

Lacing up ice skates suddenly seemed kind of sexy as Ryder crouched on his knees before me. He cupped the calf of my leg in one hand while he pushed the skate boot on my foot with the other. With cheeks flaming red, I imagined that hand sliding higher, past the bend in my knee and along the underside of my thigh. The thought made me tingle. Seeing him on his knees conjured fantasies of marriage proposals, like on a deliciously sappy Hallmark holiday movie. The twinkling Christmas lights strung around the rink certainly lent itself to the mood. With his head bent down over my feet, I could admire his thick locks of sandy colored hair. I wanted to reach out and run my fingers through it, but I had mittens on.

With a final expert tug, he tied the laces closed and looked up. "There. Tell me if it's too tight."

I wiggled my toes inside the boots. "It's fine. Since I'm from Ohio, is it really so terrible that I've never ice skated before? We have winter there too."

"No, it's not bad. It gives me an excuse to experience your first time." He stood up with one lunge of his powerful legs, his feet already encased in his own skates. "We can always adjust these later if you find they're too tight or too loose." He held out his hand. "Ready?"

I drew a big breath in, hoping the air would somehow dispel my nervousness. I didn't mind falling on my butt, I'd just rather not do it in front of him. Even if I stayed upright, I would still look ridiculous next to his practiced stride. Scratch that. Professional stride. I needed to remember just who and what this man was before I got all mushy inside.

Steeling my spine, I braced my knees. "Ready as I'll ever be."

I slipped my mittened hand into his leather gloved one. His fingers closed around it, firm and confident, and pulled me upward from the low wooden bench. It might have been my imagination, but I swore I could feel a burst of heat between our palms, even through the padding of our winter gear. It traveled up my arm and spread through my chest before crawling directly to my cheeks in a stinging blush.

Ryder took my other hand and led me toward the ice surface, our blades clomping on the semi-soft floor leading to the gate.

"One foot at a time," he said, demonstrating his step over the sill.

I followed his lead, clutching his hands tightly, and lifting each foot carefully onto the ice. So far so good – at least I was still standing.

"Oh, no!" I hissed, wobbling dangerously to the side.

"There we are." He smiled and steadied me with his firm grip. I beamed up at him as though I'd completed an important task.

He moved backward, pulling me farther into the rink. Other skaters whizzed past us at random intervals. My legs locked into a stiff, awkward stance with my knees apart but slowly glided toward him. Then the treacherous blades began to slip away, my feet jolting forward before I could stop them. As I tipped backward, Ryder's arm snaked around me and pulled me tight against him. Our upper bodies collided with a solid *whump*.

"Whoa now. Let's not have an accident before we even leave the bench." His voice was like milk chocolate to my ears – all velvety smooth and tempting. "Lean on me. I won't let you fall." His face hovered only inches above mine, and his warm breath grazed my cheek as he spoke, his words escaping to the chilly air in a puff of vapor. The man smelled like nirvana and felt like... well, I couldn't even articulate the pleasure of his weight as it pressed down on me. "Trust me."

All I could think about was the way my heart thudded, rebounding off his solid torso as my breasts pressed up against it. My legs had split and were now on either side of his in a clumsy straddle. Our pose must look hilarious to anyone watching us but gazing into the amused twinkle in his eyes I didn't care about that one bit. Trust him? I had no choice at the moment.

A path was seared by his eyes to mine. "Okay."

He gripped me by both arms and steadied me. "Don't be so stiff. Let your knees bend and take steps just like you were walking." He circled to the left to stand beside me, placing his right arm around my waist and clasping our left hands together. "Left," he said, striding with his left leg. "Right." A stride to the right. Repeat. "Left... right."

I moved my feet in sync with his, albeit not nearly as gracefully. My legs shuddered, and my blades scraped the ice in such an ungraceful pattern they sounded like rocks breaking. Clutching his hand like a lifeline, I leaned into him for support. Gradually, I found my balance, and before I knew it, we'd completed a whole lap around the rink.

"You did it." His grin was as bright as the sun. "See? Easy."

"Says the guy who plays professional hockey," I said, a little out of breath but exhilarated by the accomplishment. "It is kinda fun."

"Kinda?" he snorted, as though skating was the most fun a person could have outside of a bedroom. "Let's try it again without looking at your feet the whole time. That way, I can see your eyes."

We started off on lap number two, and to my surprise, I found that keeping my head up allowed my feet to do all the worrying and just do what came naturally. By the time we returned to the starting point, I was skating more or less on my own, only needing to hold his hand for balance. I looked up to find Ryder grinning from ear to ear.

"Pretty good for a beginner, huh?" I asked. "What's next?"

"Let's try some turns," he said and steered me toward the center of the rink where a group of artificial Christmas trees had been set up. My nervousness returned as I watched skaters weaving figure eights in and out of the sparkling fake forest and moved in close to Ryder. He didn't miss his cue, his arm slipping protectively around me again.

I felt secure as he maneuvered us between the obstacle course of plastic evergreens. He took it slow, explaining how a person could execute a turn by leaning on one edge of the blade or the other. I could feel the effect as I swayed side to side alongside him, but our path around the trees was anything but smooth. My toe picks kept getting caught on the rough ice, as the Zamboni didn't flood this area, and stumbled clumsily along despite Ryder's hold on me.

He seemed to have the patience of Job, and his gleeful laugh as he praised my valiant efforts made me laugh too. Finally, he told me to just relax my legs and let him take the lead. I figured he must be dying to speed skate after nursing me around the rink for the last hour, and happily acquiesced, showing mercy to my wobbling knees.

With expert strides, he carved his way around the trees like they were practice pylons, clutching my hand and pulling me behind like a careening caboose as he accelerated. Mindful of the other skaters, he held back on the speed, but still enough to send me swinging left and right in a game of crack-the-whip. Sounds left my lips that were somewhere between joyful hoots and terrified shrieks.

After two full passes through the course, Ryder slowed and circled back to the middle. He swung a final arc around the largest center tree, then scraped to a sudden stop. I swooped around him, my arm stretched out in full extension. My mouth hung open in a silent scream as I swept past, afraid my grip would break and send me hurtling into open ice. Instead, he reeled me in like a tuna, twirling me around underneath his arm and spinning me into his embrace. Hair and pompoms flew outward and swung in front of my eyes, blindfolding me as I landed squarely against him. He felt as solid as a statue, a rock amid the whirling maelstrom on ice.

Both his arms clamped around me, anchoring me to him. When I brushed the hair from my face, I was nearly nose to nose with my brawny, handsome instructor. He breathed heavily in and out, though he didn't seem winded in the least. As my dizziness cleared, intense pools of amber brown came into focus and stared down at me, framed by feathery, dark lashes. The sexy stubble lining his rugged jaw stood out in detail as I nestled close – dangerously, thrillingly close. Notes of his masculine and musky cologne mixed with fresh air tickled my nostrils. A familiar sensation closed in on me, the same one I'd felt at Casa Fiorino. In a strangled heartbeat, I became a trapped animal, paralyzed in willing captivity by his gaze.

His kiss descended on me with the inevitable certainty of an oncoming snowstorm. The touch of his lips swept me away like a winter wind, but his mouth enveloped me in a blanketing softness, the kiss warm and wet and exhilarating.

It seemed both brief and eternal, like having lived a lifetime in the depths of that kiss, yet felt all too short when it broke, leaving me yearning for more. I blinked as though waking from a dream state, searching Ryder's eyes for proof it had really happened.

A wink and a sexy grin told me that it had. "I've been wanting to do that since I first saw you."

A hot blush crawled up my neck for all the right reasons this time. "That was some lesson, coach."

"Hmm. And you did great. Wonder what else I can teach you?"

CHAPTER SEVENTEEN

Ryder

As promised, I ended the day with a stop at the Forager Brewery, one of my favorite spots, for a designer coffee before taking Hannah home. Getting to know her better tugged at my heartstrings. The more I talked to her – the more I liked her. I pulled up in front of the condo, again recalling my last visit here before today, and my none-too-subtle ploy to invite myself in. Major backfire. Not going there again.

"Thank you for a great day, Ryder. You've convinced me that Rochester is definitely at its best in the winter," Hannah said, her mittened hands folded politely in her lap. God, I wanted to lay her down and melt away that frozen and innocent exterior. I knew with every breath in my body that a molten hot core loomed underneath it, just waiting to be unleashed.

I nodded. "Told you so. Glad you enjoyed it."

She flashed her angelic smile that seemed to have wormed its way into my hardened heart. A smile that made my knees vibrate, and my cock swell against my fly. Unique in its dichotomous allure, saintly innocent yet sinfully beguiling. Something about this girl demanded respect... and kid gloves. I had to get her out of this car before I did something way too ahead of schedule. "Well, I've got a big day tomorrow. Let me walk you up. I need to make sure you get inside safely."

I jumped out and hustled to the passenger side to open her door, determined not to be robbed of my chance to be a perfect gentleman. I could be one when I chose and when the class and breeding of the girl inspired it. And for Hannah... I felt like I could do anything. She waited. Pulling out the latch, I held out my hand. While no red carpet led to the building entrance, I could at least pretend.

Accepting my assistance, she stepped out of the low-slung luxury seat and stood beside me. "Game tomorrow, right?"

I nodded. "And we have a morning pre-game skate. Since you know more about skating, are you up for coming to the game and giving it a try?"

She bobbed her head in the affirmative. "I think I could learn to like all things ice-related."

I took her by the elbow and guided her up the icy steps with deliberate slowness. "I'll have an access pass for you at the will-call booth. You know where that is?"

"I'm sure I can find it. Are you excited for your first professional game?"

"Of course, but not as much as I am about knowing you'll be there," I said as we reached the landing, deploying my own signature smile. Flattery usually went a long way with classy women. I was rewarded with another display of her deliciously flushed cheeks. Unbidden, I reached out to toy with a lock of her long hair, like I'd wanted to do the first night I'd seen her. Another flashback made me let it go. I wouldn't be making that mistake again, but I was reluctant to let the afternoon end. Glancing upward, I chuckled. "This is a really upscale building. I used to know someone who lived here, and I'm sure rent isn't cheap. They must pay you well at the restaurant. Maybe I'm in the wrong business."

She shook her head, pompoms flailing. "Oh, I don't rent a place here. I'm staying with family."

Curiosity unfurled in my chest. "Right. You said you were new in town. You know, I never asked where you're from in

Ohio. And I don't even know your last name."

Hannah smiled and tilted her head to the side. *Too cute for words.* "It's Robertson. Hannah Robertson, and I'm from Columbus."

"Robertson?" I said, my heart felling to my boots. "That's a coincidence – like your boss, Eloise?"

Hannah laughed. "More than a coincidence. Eloise is my sister."

The breath stalled in my lungs. "Um... wow... I didn't know that. I'll call you, Hannah."

"Thanks again for the amazing day." She gave me a flirty wave.

Mind reeling, I pecked her a quick goodbye before she ducked inside and trotted back to my car with my stomach wrapped around my feet. I slipped behind the wheel of my car and drove off.

Fuck. Fuck. *Triple Fuck.*

Her bloody *sister?* My hands clenched and unclenched the heated steering wheel in agitation as I pulled onto the highway. I didn't see much of a resemblance. Hannah's straight auburn locks compared to El's wavy brunette tresses, and her taller, slimmer frame both defied a family connection. And the face? Maybe a little around the nose and chin. Both were decidedly beautiful, but otherwise, seemed very different.

But the capability of turning into Frosty the Snowman on a dime. Check.

While guarded at first, Hannah seemed optimistic and inquisitive whereas the straight-laced, opinionated Eloise rejected everything that didn't conform to her ideals. Perhaps El just hadn't had enough opportunity to soil the blank canvas of her sister's life outlook just yet.

Give it time.

Perhaps a second date was a bad idea. Eventually, Hannah would tell Eloise about me, and there were only two outcomes. Either El would pour poison in Hannah's ear about me and make her ghost me, or Hannah would rebel and date me anyway. In that case, each minute we spent together would drive a wedge between the sisters and cause Eloise to unleash a shitstorm of destruction, with me at the epicenter.

Not a pleasant scenario.

But I liked Hannah too much to pit her against her own sister. And I wanted to see her again if only to see where it would go. Maybe we'd both find that the chemistry abated in the age-old crash and burn, and things would peter out before Eloise got involved. If not, I'd consider Eloise's discomfiture as a fringe benefit. At any rate, I had bigger things to concentrate on than women right now. Like my NHL debut tomorrow. All other worries had to be put on the backburner.

CHAPTER EIGHTEEN

Hannah

"Hanna-bee, it's so good to hear from you," Sophia said over the phone. "Have you seen Christina yet? I can hardly wait to hold her, snuggle her and inhale that baby fresh scent. That smell is like crack. I hope Phil and I can start a family soon too. Can't let Eloise always have all the attention."

"Hey, it's Auntie Hannah now, get with the program!" I said with a giggle. "Yes, I've been to the hospital a couple times already. She's gorgeous and doing well. Gaining weight and no sign of any other complications."

"Thank goodness. I'm glad we live in a day and age where preemies can thrive. El would have been heartbroken if anything went wrong with Christina. I know she'd feel like it was her fault. Even though you never let on, I'm sure she was overdoing it."

"That's El for you, taking responsibility for everything." I agreed. "Even me."

"So, how's the job going, do you like it? Is it weird working for your big sister, taking orders from her?"

My mind drifted to Casa Fiorino. "Nothing new about that, Soph. You know that as well as I do."

Sophia laughed. "Right. She's been the boss all along. How silly of me. How do you like living in Rochester? I hear it's cold."

I smiled, ready to burst with excitement over the previous day and dying to spill the beans to someone. "Oh, you just have to embrace the cold here. Rochester is at its best in winter," I quoted. "I'm even going to a hockey game tonight."

"Wow, it *must* be cold in Minnesota. Hell has frozen over if you're taking an interest in hockey," Sophia teased. "I know. You're dying to see Cole play."

Tugging my lower lip between my teeth, I fantasized about broad shoulders and chiseled jaws. "Mmm, not so much Cole, but another hockey player."

A pause. "Ohhh, so that's it. Tell me, tell me, tell me!"

Words gushed forth from my mouth, describing Ryder's good looks, smoking hot body, how he'd taught me to skate like such a perfect and attentive teacher, and of course, the *kiss*. The unfortunate events of the fundraiser had long since paled in my memory and been virtually forgotten. I left those details out of the conversation.

"He sounds wonderful, Hannah. I'm so happy that you've met someone. There's nothing quite like a first kiss. I can't wait to break the bad news to Russ," she chuckled, a touch of good-natured malice in her tone. "I can't wait to see the look on his face. Despite the fact that I'm married to his brother, he still annoys me. He's been asking about you. He even wants to come out there with Phil and me at Christmas."

My balloon of excitement deflated a little at the mention of Russ's name. No – he wouldn't dare come out here now, would he? He'd as good as told me off, not that I cared. Who did he think he was, insulting me and then thinking I'd give him a second chance? Not a snowball's chance in hell.

"Oh, are you guys able to come with Mom and Dad?" I asked, not wanting to say Russ's name out loud. "You weren't sure you could get away."

"It's still not for sure, but I'm working on it. Trying to get flights at this time of year isn't easy."

"Okay, I'll tell Eloise. She'll be thrilled to see you."

I disconnected the call and decided I wasn't about to let the remote chance of Russell Pomeroy turning up on my doorstep ruin my good mood or my evening ahead.

Since Rochester Arena wasn't far from the restaurant, I decided to walk there after work and enjoy my newfound affinity for colder weather. My lined, faux fur-trimmed pea coat had proven to be plenty warm for outdoors as well as inside ice rinks.

The arena building was hard to miss, its circular structure covering three square city blocks, the additions of a parking tower and Murphy's Finest Whiskey Pub usurping even more space. From what Eloise had told me, these extensions had caused quite an uproar in the community during their construction. I found the main entrance and got directions to the will-call window. To my surprise, a uniformed usher arrived to escort me to a plush box seat about midway up the stadium bowl. I hadn't expected a place of privilege but felt tickled to have such status because of Ryder.

The box contained four rows of six seats each, separated from the adjoining boxes by a half wall. Open railing in the front afforded a great view of the ice surface. I found my seat in the first row and settled in, awestruck by the vast space and the throngs of people filling it. I didn't realize the population of Rochester was even half that. Electronic ads raced around the perimeter of the rink in a strip of moving LED lights. The massive center clock hung from the cavernous roof above, TV images playing on all four sides above the scoreboard, its digital timer counting down to puck drop. Boy, did this town love its hockey. The atmosphere was nothing less than electric.

The box began to fill with more spectators, and the seat next to mine was soon taken by a lady wearing a fur coat. I absently wondered if it was real, as natural fur garments were rather frowned upon these days. As the woman and her friend sat down, I couldn't believe my eyes. I recognized that long mane of curly copper hair.

It belonged to Joe. Or rather, Josée.

The redhead stunner turned to me. "Hello," she said with a polite nod.

"Hello," I echoed, nonplussed. Would 'Joe' recognize me from the party? I kind of hoped not but guessed it didn't really matter.

I returned my attention to the ice, where the Detroit Wheels had already entered the rink and begun skating around. Music began to play, and the lights dimmed. A spotlight beamed down over an opening in the boards as the commentator's voice came over the PA system. "Ladies and gentlemen, please welcome your hometown Rochester Riot."

Shredder burst onto the ice first, followed by the rest of the team. The lights brightened, and the crowd's roar reached deafening proportions as the players circled one end of the rink and took their positions, some filling the players' bench and others lining up in formation at center ice. They were without their star forward tonight, since Cole had been excused from the game to be with Eloise and Christina. However, I didn't see jersey number seven.

The referee dropped the puck, and though I tried hard to follow its movement, I soon felt hopelessly ignorant of either the strategy of play or the rules of the game. The little rubber disc seemed invisible, the skater's motions my only clue to its whereabouts. It did not help my confidence that 'Joe' talked a blue streak to her friend the entire time, waving and gesturing with her fur-coated arms. If I understood any French, I might have picked up a little knowledge, but the endless stream of foreign chatter only served to irritate me. I hated feeling ignored and ignorant.

Suddenly, Joe shouted and pointed to the ice. Looking down and squinting, I saw that jersey number seven had finally made an appearance. How did they decide who came out to play and who didn't? I shook my head, wondering if I'd ever understand this complicated game, and realized that if I planned on having another date with Ryder, I'd better learn fast.

"That's the new player who won the contest," Joe said in accented English, suddenly leaning toward me. "I've met him. He's very handsome, non?"

Startled, I turned my head. "How can you tell from up here, with that helmet on?"

Josée laughed and clapped her hands. "I've seen him close up. Very close up," she said, elbowing me. "Maybe I ask him on a date after the game, so I can see him even closer. There's something to be said for being the only girl on the ice. Less competition."

A slow burn ignited my face, and not a girlish blush this time. Was Josée attracted to Ryder? That didn't make sense. Didn't he beat her out for a spot on the team? My mouth clamped shut, unable to think of any kind of response, and fixed my unseeing eyes back onto the rink. Ryder hadn't suggested anything to me about after the game, and I hadn't thought to ask. Was he the type to have more than one girl in rotation at a time? The thought dripped down from my brain and congealed around my heart like a frost. Of course, he would do that. With an extra chill, I remembered Spud calling him a 'womanizer.' Had he invited Josée here too and sat us right next to each other?

A sudden howl from the crowd snapped me to attention. The Riot had scored. Josée jumped to her feet, yelling in French.

The players circled around the net, then glided past the bench in celebration, high fiving with their gloves, Ryder in the mix. I applauded and smiled, but not quite with the fervor of the woman sitting next to me.

"Ry-der! Ry-der!" Josée chanted.

The announcer came over the PA system in a booming voice. "Riot's first goal, scored by number twenty-two, Ealon Jones... assisted by number seven, Ryder Martin!"

My heart thumped, pleased at hearing Ryder's name, but the excitement and anticipation I'd held when I'd walked into the building and actually felt special now turned into something else – a writhing nest of other, darker emotions. Doubt. Suspicion. Jealousy. I didn't like the shadow being cast across my heart.

I decided not to stay until the end. If Ryder wanted to see me again, I wouldn't be waiting at the dressing room doors. Especially if Miss French Fry would try to get there before I did so she could see him a 'little closer'. I hissed in a ragged breath, taking all my anger with it, so the negative emotion settled in my gut. I wanted none of this. Fame and fortune belonged to Eloise and Cole. All I wanted was as simple life with a man who adored me, a safe and comfortable home and our kids at my feet.

With another hiss of breath, I realized I hadn't given Ryder my phone number, nor had he asked for it. He'd have no way to contact me even if he did want to meet up later. If he even cared, my Ice Prince would just have to come to the Tower again and beg Rapunzel to let down her hair one more time. Except this time, I might cut it into a pixie before he arrived.

CHAPTER NINETEEN

Hannah

Eloise looked tired but happy when I arrived at the hospital to visit the next morning, little Christina snuggled in her arms. She greeted me with a hug and kiss. "How's the littlest Fiorino doing today?"

"Christina's doing great," El answered. "You've caught us at bonding time, only two hours each day. They say the physical contact helps speed development of her internal systems."

"Only two hours a day? I can't imagine. You must just ache to hold her round the clock," I said. "How are you and Cole managing?"

"I'm fine," El said and kissed the baby's head. "But I think my husband is going a little stir crazy. I knew he wanted to be at the game last night, although he insisted otherwise. He kept sneaking out to the lounge to catch it on TV."

"Good thing they won then. He probably would have blamed himself for a tick mark in the L column."

Eloise raised her eyebrows. "You watched the game? This Minnesota climate must be getting into your blood."

"Um, yeah. I was actually at the game," I admitted.

"Really?" Eloise queried, looking more intrigued. "That's extraordinary. What made you decide to go?"

I looked askance for a moment, wondering how much I should say, given the uncertainty in my status with Ryder, then grinned back at Eloise. I'd keep the details vague, giving just enough to keep bulldog Eloise focused on her daughter and not her single sister. "A player invited me."

"Aha. I knew you weren't telling me the whole story about the fundraiser. You caught someone's attention. Who is it?" El asked, looking excited for me.

"Well. He's brand new to the team..." I began.

El's lips pursed in thought when Christina suddenly started to fuss. "Oh, sweetheart, Mommy's here," Eloise soothed.

A nurse approached to take Christina back to the nursery. "Thank you, Jennifer," Eloise said and waved a tiny goodbye as Christina was wheeled away in her incubator unit with the nurse. She turned back to me. "Now, say again. A new player to the team? We don't have any new..." Eloise stopped short. Her brows knitted together in concern. "Oh, no. Not Ryder Martin. Tell me you don't mean Ryder Martin."

My smile faded. "Well, yes. I do mean Ryder. What's wrong with that? He seems like a decent enough guy. Lord knows he had to sacrifice everything to make it to the NHL, including his pride."

"Oh, honey," Eloise shook her head, "don't believe a word that comes out of his mouth. Stay as far away from him as you can. Please, I'm begging you. I can't be worried about you too. Not now. Not with all this happening."

What little hope remained fell back down to earth in a trainwreck of emotion. "Why? How do you know anything about him?"

"Because we worked together for years in the Riot front office, that's how. Trust me, he's not your type. And he's my age, for heaven's sake. He's too old for you. Thirty, and you're only twenty-three."

"I think I can be the judge of who's my type," I said, crossing my arms. "It was only a hockey game. Geez, El. He didn't get down on one knee. Besides, I already decided I don't want to see him again."

El blew out a breath, looking somewhat relieved. "Well, good. Keep it that way."

"Buon Giorno," came a cheerful, earthy voice from the hallway. We both turned to see Theresa enter the room, radiant as usual with her striking Mediterranean features and impeccable wardrobe. A grand lady by any standard. "How are you ladies today? Hannah, so good to see you."

"Hi, Mrs. Fiorino," I said, hugging the woman and inhaling her classy scent.

"Ah, there's two of us in the room," she replied with a grin. "Where is my little granddaughter?"

Eloise pointed. "They've just taken her back to the nursery. We can go there if you want."

Theresa Fiorino sat down between us. "In a minute. For now, I'd love to just visit with the two of you." She took Eloise's hands in hers. "Things will never be the same now that you're a mother. I think you already know that."

"Of course," El replied. "It's a whole new world. I love her so very much. It's a cellular kind of love."

Theresa clucked her tongue. "Priorities change, and you won't be able to do many of the things you used to do, at least not the same way. You always have the children to consider."

"You mean like going out for the evening?" I asked. "Don't worry. El's got a built-in babysitter. Me."

Theresa tilted her dark head back and forth. "That's one aspect, and I'm so glad she'll have you to count on as long as you're here. But you have your own path to follow, Hannah dear. Don't let family obligations dull your youthful light." She turned to El again. "Eloise, I know you're a career woman. You may not be happy with just a mother's role."

"That's why I have Casa Fiorino. I'm so lucky. I can combine career and family all in one bundle." El smiled and gave a sigh of gratitude. "Theresa, I appreciate your concern, but I think I know where my priorities lie," El assured her. "With Cole and Christina."

"I love my son, of course, and his brother, but Cole is away a lot, you know that. You'll make time for him, and he'll make whatever time he can for you and Christina." Theresa leaned forward, winking. "I will kick his butt if he doesn't. But you'll be on your own a lot. It's different for men. Their lives carry on pretty much the same after fatherhood. Women have to be stronger. Accept changes and cope with them. And let go of... control."

I listened to Theresa's words with interest. What a wise woman. She seemed to see everything and doled out some sage advice. I wondered if our own mother would say the same. "That doesn't sound very fair," I commented.

Theresa smiled at me. "Fairness has very little to do with parenthood. But it's the most rewarding and wonderful duty in the world. Nothing like it. Every woman should experience it. Such blessings change a person. For the better."

"It is a blessing," El offered, nodding.

"A blessing and a responsibility," Theresa continued. "You'll laugh, and you'll cry for your children. You'll hurt, and you'll jump for joy with them. There'll be days when you'll feel you can't do it, can't go on. And when you feel that way, remember this. Being a parent is a privilege, not a right."

After I left the hospital, my mind churned with tumbling thoughts. I hadn't expected my visit with El and Theresa to be so emotional and yet enlightening at the same time. It made me look at things from a different perspective. Theresa's insights on parenthood were profound and came from all the right places... from her heart and from experience. In silence, I sent up a prayer that El's firstborn had turned out to be a girl. I didn't think perfectionist Eloise could handle a rambunctious and messy boy during the first round. By the time her sons came, she'd be prepared.

El's admonishing comments came from experience too, but what she'd said about Ryder gave me pause. El was really, really hard on people and I didn't know exactly what my sister had against him. What was so horrible about working together in the front office? Had Ryder and El gone for the same promotion or something? If Theresa hadn't turned up, maybe I'd have heard more of the story. As much as I loved and respected Eloise, it rankled that she would presume to dictate whom I should like or not like, or what age my dates should be. Perhaps big sisters, and even bartenders didn't always know best.

As I walked past the outpatient station on my way to the main exit, I spotted a gray-haired man sitting in a wheelchair reading a magazine. I slowed my steps, thinking he looked familiar. Then it came to me – the man I'd helped into a cab at the fundraiser. I gasped inwardly. He was in bad enough shape to be in the hospital? My heart went out to him.

"Hello there," I said, walking up alongside his chair with my warmest smile. "How are you doing?"

The man started and looked up from his tabloid, *The Hockey News*. He dropped it in his lap and turned aside to stifle a cough, then regarded me with squinting eyes. His face seemed less red and grizzled than I remembered. And sober too.

"Well, pretty young lady," he said, his voice deep and scratchy. It sounded painful. "Doing okay, nice of you to ask." His look didn't suggest he remembered me.

"I'm Hannah, I work at Casa Fiorino. You were there last Friday? I hope you're feeling better." *Gah, that's silly.* If he felt better, he wouldn't be in the hospital.

The hooded eyes seemed to light up in recognition. "Oh, yeah." He put a fist to his mouth and cleared his throat with effort. "Thank you again for your help. What brings you here? Are you a nurse? That would surely make sense. Soft voice and equally soft touch."

I laughed. "A nurse? Heavens no. Just here visiting my sister."

The man nodded and attempted a smile. "Nice to have family."

"Yes, it is. I'll bet you have grandchildren coming to visit you," I said, hoping to bring a smile to his face.

He glanced down at the magazine in his lap, then seemed to stare off into the distance. "I have sons. Three of them. We don't really get along. Wife passed already."

"Oh," I said, regretting my choice of words. Good thing I wasn't a nurse. I'd be terrible at it – always forgetting to think things through.

A real nurse came out of the station and walked toward us. "Alright, Walter, they're ready for you," she said, grasping the handles of the wheelchair. "Say goodbye to your pretty friend. You're not quite up for the dating scene yet." Walter chuckled, his laugh dissolving into another uncomfortable bout of coughing.

"Goodbye, Walter," I said, stepping back as the nurse wheeled him away. I felt sorrier for the man than ever. What a pity to have a son and not have a close relationship with him. *A privilege, not a right*. Theresa Fiorino was a very wise woman.

When I arrived home, I found a courier envelope with my name and the building address on it taped to the mailbox bank. My heart constricted at the thought it might be from Franklin University. After detaching the seal, I turned it over in shaking hands. I didn't recognize the originating address.

Willing down my anxiety, I took the elevator up to our unit before opening it. Once inside, amid the sanctuary of El's massive houseplant conservatory, I tore it open only to reveal another plain white envelope, the size of a greeting card. Both relieved and disappointed, I pulled the flap and slid out a note card with a glossy photo on the front. I stared in confusion. A blonde model wearing an elegant, vintage evening dress.

As I opened the card, my breath caught. This was better than any news from any school. The blank interior contained a handwritten note and a five-hundred-dollar gift card from HERS, a chic clothing store in downtown Rochester.

Hannah,

You said there was no way to make up for that dress. Maybe this can help?

I missed you after the game. Since I'm such a dufus, I forgot to put you in my contacts.

I know you're way smarter than me, so perhaps you'll dial mine instead.

I really want to see you again. Hopefully in a fantastic dress.

-Ryder

His cell phone number followed at the bottom of the note. A debilitating flutter started in my chest, and my tongue felt thick in my throat. If this man was a womanizer, he knew how to make a girl weak in the knees. But my heart refused to believe it. This gesture was far too personal, too thoughtful and generous to be just another page from some Casanova's *Pocket Guide to Panty Removal*. No man shelled out half a grand just to spread a woman's legs. He wanted to get to know me better. He really cared, and I felt as though I could fly around the room with that knowledge as a jet pack.

Eloise is wrong about him. She is.

I dialed the number before my feet could touch ground again.

"Hello?"

Something twisted low in my belly at the gravelly sound of his voice. "Hi. It's the smartest girl in Rochester calling. And the luckiest. Thank you for the card."

His laugh came across as a low, sexy rumble, as though he'd just woken up. It might as well have been a six point five on the Richter scale, shaking my soul to its foundation.

"You're welcome," he said, the sly smile forming on his face as visible to me as if he'd been standing in the room. Even though my heart told me he was sincere, a part of me still doubted him due to El's careless words. "If it makes you happy, that's all that matters. Did you enjoy the game?"

"You got an assistant," I said. "I don't know much about hockey, but I know that was a good thing. Congratulations."

He laughed. A big, booming sound that sent moisture flooding my panties as my heart whomped against my ribs. "Mmm, actually, it's called an assist. A pass to the goal scorer in this case. I was wondering what else I could teach you besides skating. Guess I've found my answer."

I smiled and bit my lip, daring myself to ask the next question. "So when's my next lesson, coach?"

"About hockey?"

CHAPTER TWENTY

Ryder

I disconnected the call, closed my eyes, and leaned my head back on the pillow. My happy grin remained in place, and the sweet tones of Hannah's voice lingered in my ear. A nice way to be roused from sleep. Picturing her naked and splayed out next to me, prepared to indulge my every naughty thought gave me the inspiration to deal with my typical morning wood. Now *there* was something I'd be happy to teach her.

Except it wasn't morning. My phone said two-fifteen p.m. I'd laid down for a nap after returning from my trip to the mall to pick out the card and gift for her. I'd pretty much gone straight home after the game last night. Though my body was in top condition, the mental stress and anxiety building up over the weeks of tryouts had taken their toll. I felt tapped out.

It did feel a little weird being home in the middle of a weekday. I'd been an office guy for so long, it would take some getting used to not having an eight to five schedule. But I'd best not get too used to it just yet. Staring the wrath of Sheehan Murphy straight in the face, Kristoff had begrudgingly signed off on a month's leave of absence while I pursued my dream. If the Riot didn't offer me a contract, I'd be back behind that desk in a matter of weeks, trying to yank the chain off the concrete ball.

Hell no. I forced my doubts and that disagreeable picture away and replayed my minutes on the ice in my mind. On my first shift, I'd proven himself – made a meaningful contribution to the team by setting up Jones for that goal. It led to more ice time, only nine minutes in total but not bad for an untried player. Rookies sometimes didn't even get that. I'd shown them, shown them all. They had to give me that contract.

They had to. And to cement the deal, I'd give them everything. Lay it all out on the ice. So much that there could only be one outcome.

A permanent place in the NHL for Ryder Martin – world's oldest rookie.

I was scheduled to play the remaining two home games before Christmas break, and my performance would either make it or break it. Though I wanted to explore this relationship with Hannah, I had to put all my focus into the team now. Nothing could distract me from that, even the lure of her sweet innocence. Her kiss held the promise of better things to come, there was no need to rush. Besides, she seemed perfectly content to take things slow and I would honor that pace.

For now, I could fantasize. As I moved to ease my aching hard-on, I wondered what kind of underwear she fancied. Thongs? Lacy little push-up bras with front closures? Even better, thigh highs and garters? Yeah. Like that. The kind I could snap open with one hand and pull the skimpy fabric from between her lovely round ass cheeks with my teeth. Then spank her and tell her what a bad girl she was. And show her how she could be even much, much naughtier under my expert guidance.

CHAPTER TWENTY-ONE

Hannah

"I can't believe you guys are home! Oh, let me see her," I squealed, helping Eloise in the door with her bags and belongings. The most important package came in the form of Christina herself, safely swaddled inside her industrial-grade baby carrier. The Fiorinos clearly would spare no expense when it came to quality children's accessories.

They could certainly afford it.

His Riot ball cap askew, Cole shuffled in behind Eloise, carrying gift bags and flower arrangements they'd received from friends while still at Mayo.

"Holy shit," he said. "Who knew having a baby entailed impersonating a UPS man? Everyone knows that brown is not my color."

Despite his complaints, I could tell he was going to be one star-struck daddy, hopelessly under the spell of his own little princess. Her first headwear was sure to be a tiara – one that would fit underneath a hockey helmet.

By happy coincidence, they got the green light for Mom and baby to come home on December sixteenth, Eloise's birthday.

"What a great birthday present," I said as El set the carrier down. I crouched and peered under the bright colored canopy to see Christina sleeping peacefully under several layers of covering. Sprigs of black hair that stuck out from under a knitted bonnet framed her tiny face. "Sweet dreams little monkey," I whispered, "welcome home." I stood to give Eloise a hug. "And to you too. Happy Birthday, sis. I'm sorry I didn't get you a present yet."

"Thanks, Hanna-bee. No worries. The only gift I want right now is a long hot bath."

"I'll run it for you," I said. "Bubbles, I presume?"

She nodded, a weary look creasing her brow. "Please."

I scurried down the hall to the master bath to start the water running, passing the nursery that had formerly been Eloise's home office. I hoped El and Cole would find a house they liked soon because I felt guilty taking up the extra guest room.

I poured a generous capful of El's favorite coconut-scented bubble bath into the filling tub and lit the candles that ringed the ledge. When the foamy clouds of suds almost spilled over, I twisted the taps closed and turned to leave the room.

Eloise stood in my path, eyes flashing.

"What is this," El asked, holding up the fancy greeting card that Ryder had sent me.

I flinched inwardly. "Just a card. Sorry, I thought I'd put it in my room."

"It *was* in your room. I went to put some of my flowers in there for you and saw it on the dresser. Why is Ryder Martin sending you notes about dresses via private courier and giving out his phone number?" El cocked her head, waiting for an answer. Her green eyes sported a look that I hadn't seen in years. *The Inquisition.* Though I shrank before it out of habit, something else lit inside of me now. Something resembling anger.

"That's my business, not yours. I can't believe you read it. That's private." I reached out and snatched the card from Eloise.

El dropped her now-empty hand to her hip. "I thought you said you weren't seeing him."

I cast my eyes aside and moved past my sister into the bedroom. "I wasn't. Then. I didn't lie, and I'm not hiding anything from you."

Eloise followed. "But you're thinking of changing your mind? Why? I told you to steer clear of that arrogant jackass. He's only out for one thing, Hannah. I thought you valued yourself more than as a cheap lay for the Riot's new token player. Let him go defile some cheap slut and not my sister."

Why is she doing this? We haven't fought since I was a teenager. Stomach in knots, I turned on her. "He's not an asshole. What did he do to you that made you hate him so much?"

"Fortunately, nothing," Eloise fumed, her voice raised, "but he sure wanted to. He thinks he can buy his way into a girl's pants. I showed him differently. And over my dead body is he going to get into my baby sister's with some extravagant gesture. Christ, he's trying to transact for your pussy like a john seeking a high-end prostitute."

I blanched at the harsh words coming from my sister's mouth. This wasn't like Eloise at all to be so crass. She must be overly stressed and tired, so despite my hurt at the words, I tried to cut El some slack. But even if I was only a freeloading relative, I didn't need to be lectured, and I didn't need my privacy invaded. I didn't want to be mad either, but I couldn't push it all back down.

"Your post-natal hormones must be kicking in, El," I argued, putting a hand on my jutting hip and flinging my hair back for good measure. "Remember you're Christina's mother, not mine."

A shuffling noise at the bedroom door broke our standoff. We both spun to see Cole standing there, holding his cell phone in one hand and Christina cradled in the other.

He looked awkwardly between us. "Sorry... the real estate agent just called. That house we saw last month down in Scenic Oaks has come on the market. We need to put an offer in like, fast. That is if that's still okay with you, sweetie? I know we talked about building, but with the stress of Christina's early birth, I'm thinking..."

Eloise gave me one last piercing look before moving toward the bathroom. "That's great news, babes. It really is time to move. And you're right. I don't want the stress of a new build and dealing with an architect and a contractor. We can do that later on down the line, once you retire and we find our forever home city."

I stalked away to my own room, flopping onto the bed, hot tears ready to spill onto my pillow. I knew I'd wear out my welcome eventually but didn't want it to come to this – fighting and arguing. On El's birthday too with an infant in the condo. And only a few weeks until Christmas. Our parents would be arriving soon, then we'd really be jammed in here like sardines. I'd likely be relegated to the couch unless Mom and Dad opted for a hotel. Might be a good idea, even better if I stayed there myself. I could already hear my dad's voice ringing in my ears, gruff with his disapproval again.

Damn. I rolled over onto my back, frustrated. The coming New Year didn't look so bright for me. Unless...

I couldn't stop my thoughts from drifting to Ryder. Now that he had my number he'd called and texted me several times, though we hadn't really seen each other since our skating date. His chance to play for the Riot was far too important, the final decision looming. It was enough to know that he thought of me often and wanted to reach out. Though angry with her, I now understood El's situation, having to share her man with his sport. And I'd been right about something else. Once you fell for someone, the heart took over, and it had no ears for criticism.

I reached for my cell phone and scrolled through my contacts, my finger hovering over his name. After punching it in, I listened to it ring.

"Hey," he answered. *Oh, I can listen to that bedroom-y voice all day long.* I felt near melting every time I heard it.

"Hey, am I disturbing you?"

"Never. What's up?"

"It's..." I heaved a giant sigh.

"Whoa," he said. "That sounded like the entire golf dome tent deflating. What's wrong?"

"Nothing."

He chuckled and the low rumble caused my belly to contract. "Oh, please. Never say 'nothing' to a man. We all know it means 'something' and it's never good. Tell me."

"I had an argument with Eloise."

He laughed aloud this time. "No shit. Who hasn't? She's an argument on legs. I swear, if Christ himself came down from Heaven, she'd give him an earful about his litany of faults."

I didn't find it that funny. Our connection was still too new for him to go after my family, even though El had annoyed me too. "So I take it you've had arguments with her?"

"Hell, yes. We used to work together. If you think she's bossy at home around people she loves, imagine what she's like with her subordinates."

My heart ached even at the hint of a war between two people I cared about. "Yeah, she mentioned that you've had words before. And she said other things too."

Silence hung over the connection for a heartbeat or two. "Like what?" he asked, his voice quiet.

No. I didn't want to confront him with El's accusations, and let our fight ruin the one thing that felt bright and good in my life right now. Maybe El didn't know Ryder the way I did, since my sister didn't excel at giving people second chances. Or even first chances for that matter. "That you're too old for me."

I heard him take a few breaths, then make a clucking noise. "Well, I'm twenty-nine. How old do I need to be before I'm too old for you? We were both born in the same damn decade."

It was my turn to snicker as I thought of Walter and his nurse's cracks about his age. "Older than that."

"Good to know I have a few years left before I reach my expiration date."

"You sound like you're talking about moldy cheese." I pressed my ear closer to the phone, wanting to feel closer to him. My anger at El faded away on the buttery softness of Ryder's flirtatious voice. "How young do I have to be before I'm too young for you?"

"Well, since we're playing twenty questions, how young are you? Way too young to be an aunt, I say."

It seemed an odd way to phrase the question, how young as opposed to how old, but it made me smile. "I'll be twenty-four in March."

"Oh heavens to Murgatroyd, that's nearly a six-year gap. How will we ever communicate?" he said melodramatically. "Would it help ease your mind if I called Aflac and purchased some supplemental insurance?"

The laugh came from deep inside where a little bit of light had seeped into the darkness caused by Eloise. "I suppose I could learn to decipher stone tablets and operate an abacus."

"Hey now, let's not get nasty," he chuckled. "Feel better?"

"Yeah. I just feel a little crowded right now. El and Cole brought Christina home today, and my mom and dad are arriving week after next. I feel like I'm in the way. I lack...

space."

"Christina, huh? Very Italian. I didn't realize you were all squeezed into that condo. No wonder you're cranky. With his mega salary, I'm surprised Cole is content living in El's condo."

"Well, they've been looking for a house for ages, and it sounds like they've found one now. The agent called earlier this evening."

"Good for them. Moving is a pain in the ass though," Ryder said. "Sounds to me like you need a little escape."

"Hmm," I scoffed. "Escape to where?"

He paused. "Listen, I'm sorry I haven't been able to take you on another date. This is my one chance to live my dream, and I can't let anything break my focus. It's only for a little bit longer."

I twirled a lock of my hair around my finger. "I understand how important hockey is to you. You don't have to apologize."

"Maybe not, but I want you to know that you're important to me too. Even if my twenty-nine-year-old ass can't keep up with a young whipper-snapper like you."

Important to him? My heart did a backflip. Did he really mean it, or did he just know all the right words to say through his years of playing the game?

"I have an idea," he went on. "After our game on the twenty-second, I have nothing to do but wait for the team's decision after New Year's. How about we take a little trip between Christmas and New Year's? It would get you out of that condo."

"A trip?" I said, hoping I'd heard right. "Where?"

"I thought maybe up north. Do you ski?"

"About as much as I skate," I admitted. "Not many mountains in Ohio."

"No problem. One more thing I can teach you. Are you up for a couple days of... education?"

"Oh Ryder, I don't know. With my job and my parents coming and everything…"

"Yeah, okay," he said, sounding a bit bummed. *Didn't he have family to visit at Christmas too?* "I'll check into some bookings, and if you can tear yourself away from the restaurant and your family, we can make it work. When do your folks leave?"

"They're only staying a few days. Why don't you check the day after Christmas since it falls on a Tuesday this year? Weekdays are always slower at Casa. I'm sure I can slip away since I haven't taken any days off since I got here."

I'd never gone away with a boyfriend before. This was new territory. Grown-up territory. Wasn't that what I wanted all along? Wasn't that why I'd come to Rochester to spread my wings and fly? Suddenly, it occurred to me that he could just as easily invite Josée Thibault on a ski rendezvous – and I would bet she wouldn't say '*non.*'

"I'd like to go with you," I said in a rush before I could change my mind and retreat back into my old habits. "I'm a big girl - I can do what I want."

"Right," he said, and I heard satisfaction and something else – relief? – lacing the words. "That's *my* big girl talking."

CHAPTER TWENTY-TWO

Hannah

Eloise reached up to hug our dad as his big frame eased through the door. "Merry Christmas, Dad," she said, planting a kiss on his cheek. "Mom." She turned to our mother as she stepped in behind him, encircling her in an equally big bear hug. "Merry Christmas."

"Hi, Dad," I said, exchanging places with Eloise.

"Hi, Princess," he said, wrapping his large arm around my shoulders. "How are you doing out here with El and company? Behaving yourself?"

"I am. Super busy with the restaurant and Christina and, well everything. You guys are a day early... what happened?"

"Where is that little angel?" Mom cooed, looking around. "I can't wait to meet our first grandchild. And a girl to boot. I'm so happy!"

"There's your answer," Dad said, gesturing to his wife. "Grandma was getting so antsy I had to beg an extra day off work."

"Here she is," Cole's voice called as he approached from the living room, carrying Christina in his arms.

"Merry Christmas, Mom," I said, giving my mother a quick hug. "Let me take your coat."

"Thank you, sweetheart," she said, her palm lingering on my cheek. "Is everything okay with you? You look pale."

I nodded. "Yes, just fine. Go and hold Christina," I said, hanging my parent's coats in the hall closet. I started to roll the three big suitcases they'd brought down the hall toward my bedroom when my dad stopped me.

"That green one, bring it here, Hannah," he said. "It's full of presents."

Mom's eyes brightened. "Oh, yes. We've brought gifts from Sophia and Phil too, since they decided they couldn't come out with us after all. Expensive flights for newlyweds and all that." She turned back to the baby in her arms. "Just look at you," she cooed, placing a fingertip on her tiny nose. "So much like Cole with all that thick, black hair."

"Really?" El asked, standing next to Mom. "Theresa thought she looks more like me."

"Girls always seem to favor their fathers. All of you looked like your dad when you first entered this world," she said, glancing up at us and then at Dad. "But as you grew older, you could see a resemblance to both parents."

I wheeled the green suitcase over near the Christmas tree that me and El had decorated only a few days ago. A baby in the house sent everyone's schedule into chaos, including grandparents who lived hundreds of miles away. Their early arrival presented a problem. It was the Riot's last home game tonight, and of course, Cole had to be there. I wanted to go too, I'd promised Ryder, but El would expect me to stay and visit with Mom and Dad. I wasn't about to reveal to her why attending the game was so important. I'd only get my ass chewed out again without any relevant facts being presented to support her case.

When they moved into their new house, I'd already decided I wouldn't go with them, whether I got accepted to online grad school at Franklin or anywhere. It was high-time I made it on my own. An independent woman.

With Christina handed off to Dad, Mom opened the suitcase

and started unloading all the wrapped packages inside it, passing them to me to place under the tree. She pulled out a smallish box with bright red foil wrapping and a fancy bow that had gotten a bit crushed in transit. Mom fluffed and straightened it, then handed it over carefully. "This is for you."

I met my mother's eyes and reached for it. "Aw, thanks. Mom."

Mom beamed. "It's from Russ."

The box seemed to freeze in my hands, turning my fingertips cold. "I don't want it," I said quietly, passing it back as if it were laced in arsenic. "Why would you bring this?"

"It's just a little token." She frowned and shoved it back at me. "Russ likes you. He asked us to bring it. There's no harm in opening it. I think he feels bad about the wedding. He was wearing a very guilty look when he gave me this. Did something happen between the two of you?"

"You want me to like him, don't you?" I asked, finally coming to a realization. "I don't. I won't. Accepting this is as good as lying. There will *never* be anything between Russ and me. I don't have any romantic interest in him. In fact, I don't even think he's a nice person."

Mom threw her hands up in the air. "Hannah, whatever has gotten into you? Where are you Midwestern manners? I'm not sending it back. It will hurt his feelings."

"What about my feelings?" I argued, crossing my arms over my chest. No way could I tolerate being treated like an naughty child for days on end by every damn Robertson in this condo. "Or am I not supposed to have any? You're more worried about Russ's feelings than your own daughter's!"

My mother clucked her tongue. "We're worried about you, dear. You can't work in a restaurant the rest of your life, and if you're not going to go to grad school then, well, maybe you should think about getting married to someone who can take care of you, who has his own means."

"Someone like Russ, for instance?" I didn't want to believe I was hearing this fifties bullshit from my own mother. The woman who'd given me life and was supposed to have my best interests at heart – my happiness too – and was supposed to love me unconditionally. "Did Dad put you up to this?"

She gave a small shake of her head and placed her hand on my arm. "It doesn't have to be Russ. We just want you to think more seriously about your future. I'm not trying to upset you."

My heart squeezed in my chest. "No? Well, you're doing a good job of it."

"Okay, I'm sorry... let's not argue about it now. We're here to enjoy Christmas together."

"I'm sorry, too," I said, taking my mom's hand. "I seem to be a disappointment to everyone lately. Or maybe always."

CHAPTER TWENTY-THREE

Ryder

Only forty-two point four seconds remained on the clock. With the visiting Barracudas ahead four goals to three, scoring the game's tying point was likely the best outcome the Riot could hope for, forcing the game into overtime. I'd skated a few shifts early in the game, but mostly rode the bench in the third period. Tamping down my anxiety, I watched my teammates pressure the Barracudas in their end, desperately looking for a stay of execution with a timely netter.

Clustered traffic in front of the opposing goal turned ugly as Fiorino's shot found its way through and rebounded off their stellar goalie, Aaron Dell. Shooters and defenders both jammed at the loose puck. I lost sight of it amid all the bodies. I'd always hated those greasy moments inside the blue paint, they were dangerous for both sides.

A whistle sounded, and all eyes locked on the referee. Instead of the hoped-for goal, the official signaled a penalty to San Jose. *Fuck yeah.* Here was our golden chance to tie it up. McTaggart cued Shredder out of the net, and to my surprise, tapped me on the shoulder.

"Get out there for the extra attacker," Shane said.

Stunned, I wasted no time, launching myself over the boards and streaking toward the face-off circle inside the Barracuda's zone. We'd done plenty of specialty team drills during practice, but as a D-man I'd mostly been on the kill side. McTaggart said they wanted a two-way player. If I proved solid on the power play, it could seal the deal for me.

Pulling the goalie meant a slightly different kind of power play, however. Winning the draw was imperative. The opposing team could not be allowed to gain control of the puck, period. Cole didn't disappoint us. He swept the puck to his winger who immediately passed it to his D in the high slot. He rifled it across, and I caught it on the square on my tape. I turned and fired it down low to the forwards on my side. They dished off between them, looking for the hole, but the Barracuda's defense was on us like stink on shit.

We maneuvered the puck free and sent it back to the blue line. In one motion, I caught the pass and directed it to my partner on the opposite side. We were trained to never watch the clock, but players developed an inner sense of how much time remained, and I knew it was slipping away fast.

My D fired it back down low, Jones picking it up and throwing a centering pass in front of the crease. A Barracuda's stick interrupted and popped it straight out up middle ice, losing precious milliseconds. Another Riot forward reached it before it left the zone, shoveling it to the far D who then fired it to me. No more time for us to scramble for it down low. I wound up. In my vision, the puck moved toward me in ultra-slow motion despite its speed upward of eighty miles per hour and blasted a hail-Mary slapper toward the net.

The high-pitched 'tink' of metal echoed in my ears.

The breath stalled in my lungs.

I stared at the mass of players blocking my view, looking for the sign, the arms and sticks raised in triumph. And I did. In Barracuda jerseys.

My heart felt like it would explode as I saw the referee's striped arms winging outward. No goal. The puck had bounced out instead of in, and to my further horror, saw it hurtling out of the melee straight toward Shredder's empty net. Pivoting on a dime, I chased it down, catching it with feet to spare but heard the disheartening wail of the horn just as my stick touched it.

Fuck.

I swept it toward center ice where the linesman picked it up. A literal swarm of Barracuda's circled, savoring the taste of blood as they celebrated in front of their own bench.

I trooped to the dressing room alongside my dejected teammates but felt more than one kind of loss. The horn had signaled not only the end of the game but possibly the end of a journey. I'd done all I could, left it all on the ice. The rest wasn't up to me.

After the coach's debrief and donning our street clothes, the players began to leave the arena for a well-deserved holiday break. For me, it wouldn't be an entirely relaxing one. Now that the fate of my hockey career was out of my hands, all the other concerns I'd held at bay came rushing in like a busted dam.

With my mom long gone and disconnected from my father and brothers, Christmas hadn't been much of an occasion to celebrate in the last ten years or so. I typically went away for a few days if the calendar worked out, pretty much not thinking about anything or anybody. But I had plenty to think about this year – my father languishing with a terminal disease, my career on the brink of either stratospheric high or status quo low.

I switched on my phone as I walked down the hall to the exits. I always turned it off while on the ice – no distractions. It buzzed to life with a flurry of emails and texts, one in particular bringing a grin to my face.

Hannah: Hey... sorry couldn't be there, something came up... call me later?

Me: You at home?

Hannah: yes watched game on TV... you were brilliant
Me: ha-ha... did my best... call you in a bit

I pocketed the device until I could get to the privacy of my car and call her. I kinda figured she wouldn't come. Home games started late in the evenings, and it wasn't much of a date when a couple basically couldn't be in the same room at the same time – and one of them sweating for three hours on the ice beforehand.

"Hey, Martin," I heard from up ahead. "You coming?"

I looked up to see Jones and a few others gathering by the entrance to the connecting walkway between the rink and the event center. "Where?"

"We're gonna crash Murphy's pub for some Christmas cheer. The stingy fucker owes us big time. At least three each. Top shelf." The guys all laughed. "Join us?"

I thought about it. What the hell. I had nothing else on the docket, and I could find a corner somewhere inside and call Hannah from the bar. I hadn't been inside Murphy's Finest for a while. Kristoff went there a lot, trolling for the classy corporate types he loved to hook up with and occasionally invited me, but I avoided being seen socially with the boss. He and Murphy seemed to prefer each other's exclusive company anyway.

The group of players walked in and commandeered a table with a view. Patrons still filled the VIP section, but the main room had emptied of the majority of spectators. After the heartbreaking loss, I hoped we didn't get heckled by the disgruntled. Especially me, since I was essentially still an outlier. I didn't have the loving support of the Riot fans as of yet. Maybe never. I sighed and then ordered a beer and the obligatory shot of Irish whiskey alongside. I didn't love the stuff, but it made sense to imbibe the owner's product in his own establishment.

I hit up Hannah in my contacts and waited for her to answer.

"Hi," she said, her voice sounding more anxious than usual.

"Hi. Got your message. What's up?"

"Sorry I couldn't come to the game. My parents arrived a day early, and since Cole had to be there, I couldn't very well leave too. I didn't want to–"

"Have to explain to your sister?" I said, finishing her sentence. "I get it. Don't poke a sleeping bear."

She let out a sigh, the kind I hoped to hear right next to my ear when I finally got her sweet, tight body into bed and brought her to climax for the very first time. I couldn't wait to see the color of those blue eyes in that moment.

"I don't care about that anymore. I really want to go skiing with you after Christmas, and I'll tell her so... that is, if the invitation is still open?"

I turned and looked out the panoramic windows so the guys couldn't see my face as I smiled nor overhear my conversation. "You bet. I made the reservations already, and it's at least a five-hour drive. I'll pick you up on the twenty-sixth around eight a.m., sound good?"

"Wow, the day after?"

I chuckled into the phone. "Yeah, I thought you said it was okay as long as it wasn't during a busy time at the restaurant. Are you already getting cold feet?"

A pause. "Oh, I guess I thought..."

My heart flipped over. What the hell did this woman want from me? I'd followed her instructions to the letter. "Thought what? That you'd be waiting up for Santa with milk and cookies? I thought you weren't under your father's thumb anymore. Do you want to come with me or not?"

After the words broke free of my mouth, I hesitated and chided myself. The night's loss and my resulting uncertainty had wound me up a bit, and I kept forgetting that Hannah was really close to her family and most likely worried about disappointing those she loved. This would probably be her first time away from them at the holidays. But fuck – it wasn't like I'd asked her to leave over Christmas Eve or Day when normally, I'd be away from home starting on the 23rd, drowning my loneliness in beer and sports. I'd made the whole thing completely her decision.

Silence reigned for a few seconds before she spoke. "Yes, of course I do. It's just that... I don't have any ski clothes. I thought I could go shopping for some after Christmas when there are really good sales."

Play your cards right, and you won't need any clothes, baby girl.

"News flash. Santa's got a brand-new bag, honey. Climb in, or you'll miss the ride. There's a pro shop at the hill. Don't worry about it, let's just go and have fun, okay? You know, Hannah, it's hard to leave your family – especially your new niece, but I promise to make it worth your while. We haven't had that much time together either. Stop overthinking things and give yourself the ultimate present. The gift of knowing your own mind and making your own decision."

"Okay."

"Okay. Talk soon."

After swiveling in my chair, I nearly dropped my phone. Across from me, between Jones and Bennett sat none other than Tiny 'Joe' Thibault, her mass of curly red hair virtually aglow in the moody bar lighting shining down on her head. "Allo, Ryder. That was a great shot. Bad luck, eh?"

I pocketed the phone and shifted in my chair, straightening my jacket and tie in the process. I really, really didn't need the contest's runner-up observing and commenting on my performance. Even if she looked hot as hell in that cream-colored shift dress with spaghetti straps.

"Yeah. Bad luck." I shrugged. "History now. You staying in Rochester for the holidays? I thought you'd want to be home in Saskatoon by now."

Josée pursed her lips as the guys around me started to chuckle. She leaned forward, the neck of her dress showing a bit more of her freckled chest than it should. "Say it with me," she said. "Sas-ka-chew-ahn."

"Sas-ka-chew-ahn," we all mimicked in unison.

Our drinks arrived, and I picked up my snifter of Murphy's. "I'll drink to that," I said, then downed it in one gulp.

"I have a few friends here," Josée went on. "They're throwing a New Year's party so, *oui,* I stay there 'til then. Warmer here than La Ronge."

"Didn't think anywhere could be colder than here," Bennett said. "I'm a California boy, and I can tell you I'm freezing my ass off up here. Where I come from, they don't even sell winter coats."

Josée's head swiveled back and forth as she observed each of the men surrounding her. Taking a swig of my beer, I watched the long silver strings of her earrings dangle as she moved. Definitely a looker, and would score high on the four F scale, but not exactly my type. Women athletes were a little too muscular for my taste. I liked soft and supple curves. A handful of womanly flesh everywhere my hands could stray.

"Say, never did hear who put in the highest bid for you at the auction," I said. "Who's the lucky man?" I glanced over at Jones who gave me the finger. "Aw, some asshole outbid you, Ealon? Told you so." General snickers sounded around the table.

"A local businessman," Josée said, lifting her glass of wine to her lips and taking a sip. "We only spoke once since the auction. Haven't decided where we're going yet."

My eyes scoped the table, the guys all looking like canary-stuffed cats. With a sigh, I turned my hands palm up. "Who?"

"Spencer Davies," Josée said. "Do you know him?"

I swallowed hastily, to avoid choking on my mouthful of brew. "Spud? Spud won the bid?" I laughed out loud. *Didn't see that one coming.* "Snooze you lose, guys." I set my beer aside and stood up, heading for the men's room. I checked my phone again for messages but noted nothing important other than the time. Twelve forty-five a.m. Shit. As good as a cold beer tasted after a game, I should get home.

I exited the washroom a few minutes later, intending to return to the table and say my farewells. With a pang of regret, I realized I might not see these guys again, at least not as teammates and on such an intimate basis. Discarding the negative thought, I continued on my way. When I reached the end of the hall leading back to the lounge, a figure stepped into my path.

"Ryder," she said, grabbing my arm. "Merry Christmas." Josée reached up and planted a kiss on my lips, then tried to shove her warm tongue inside my mouth. At one time, I might have taken the offering with gratitude, but now, only one woman occupied my thoughts and stirred my body. Hannah. She belonged to me already and I wouldn't betray her. Joe's brazen antics gave a whole new meaning to French kiss.

"Whoa," I said, pulling away. "Merry Christmas to you too... but what...?"

Before I could say anymore, she placed a finger to my lips and tucked a cocktail napkin in my jacket pocket. Her teasing green eyes locked on mine.

"I like you," she whispered. "I like a man who challenges me. Who can keep up with me. I want to fuck you. Call me."

CHAPTER TWENTY-FOUR

Hannah

"You're what?"

"I'm going skiing with a friend," I said as I continued placing clothes and toiletries into my small carry-on case, ignoring the underlying implication of my sister's indignant question.

Eloise stood in the doorway to the guest room, looking as though she was about to cry. "It's the day after Christmas. Mom and Dad came all this way to see us. You can't just take off. What about the after Christmas sales Mom loves so much? Jesus, Hannah. Why have you started being so rebellious and disappointing everyone?"

I felt a strong stab of guilt, but the need to assert my independence pressed even stronger against my rigid back, shoving me forward toward what I actually wanted for a change. And disappointing everyone? I'd been doing nothing but catering to Eloise's every whim since I'd arrived. "I've seen everyone, we had a great few days together, and I'm likely going to be back to Columbus soon anyway. Mom and Dad are here to see you, Cole, and Christina. Not me. And since when do you buy off the rack?"

"Since I moved to Minnesota," El said. "Since when do you ski?"

"I can learn, can't I?" I asked, flashing a smile I hoped would soften the moment. "I've been learning a lot of new things since I've been in Rochester, and I'm finding that I like stepping outside my comfort zone. Besides, we're pretty cramped in here, admit it. Everyone's on top of each other. This will give you more space, more time to visit with them."

Eloise frowned. For the first time ever, things had been tense between us. I didn't like it one bit, it felt cold and weird, but I also didn't like the way Eloise decided she had the right to butt into my private life. Some distance apart would do us both good.

"Do I know this friend?" El asked, one eyebrow raised. "When will you be back?"

I chewed the inside of my mouth for a few seconds, deciding how best to answer. I didn't actually know the details of where we were going or how long we planned to stay. I just trusted Ryder to make the arrangements.

"Yes, it's someone you know. And we'll be back in a couple days."

El pursed her lips, clearly biting back the words she had in mind. "Hanna-bee, you're not fooling anyone, least of all me. You haven't made any friends in Rochester. I know who you're talking about, and I'm warning you. Do. Not. Do This. You barely know him, and you're going away with him, alone?" Her voice turned from petulant to pleading. "You don't know what you're doing. What if he does something... inappropriate?"

I can only hope he does something you'd deem inappropriate.

"I do know what I'm doing, El," I said, exasperated. I was doing something selfish for a change. Something I deserved. I turned to face her. "I'm not a kid anymore. I thought I proved that to you by working in the restaurant all this time. Can't I have a little fun for a change? You said I was your rock, that I was strong. Now, I need a break. Didn't you mean it?"

Eloise's shoulders sagged a little as she stepped closer. "Of course I meant it. I never say things I don't mean, so please listen to what I'm going to say to you." She looked me in the eyes, her sincerity and love showing through her penetrating gaze. "Ryder Martin is a predator. He's only interested in one thing. Sex. He'll seduce you, get you into bed, then put a notch on his stick and move on to the next willing victim. Don't be one of them, I'm begging you, Hannah. When he breaks your heart, it will break mine. I can't stand to see pain in your gorgeous eyes."

I almost trembled in the wake of El's damning words. She was deadly serious and clearly desperate to protect me, like she always had. She would never stop trying to protect me, I understood that now. It was like trying to stop my heart from beating. But I didn't need protecting any longer and knew that part of El's behavior stemmed from postpartum chemistry. Our mom had even said so.

"El," I said, gripping her gently by the arms. "I hear you. I love you. I trust you. But I trust Ryder too. He's not like you say. He's been nothing but a gentleman to me. We've been seeing each other a while now – so it's time to ease up. I know you want to protect me, but you can't do it forever. Even if something happens, isn't a broken heart a female rite of passage? Allow me to live my life and take my own journey. Besides, you have someone else who needs your protection now. It's time for you to trust me. Can you do that? Please?"

My sister relaxed her stance and gave a reluctant nod. "You're right. I can't protect you forever. But Hannah..."

"What?"

"Trust your feelings too. If you feel something isn't right, or you're asked to do something you don't want to do, don't ignore your gut. And use protection. Promise?"

I crossed my fingers over my heart. "Promise."

"Okay." El took a deep breath and pushed her hair back from her face. "Are you at least going to stay for breakfast? Mom's made her famous biscuits and gravy. She'll be disappointed if you don't have some. You're so skinny, she's accused me of not feeding you enough."

I sighed and gave in. "Sure."

We all settled in around the dining table, Christina's carrier on its own chair between Eloise and our mom. We'd all woken early. Me because Ryder wanted to hit the slopes today and the others because Christina's wailing flowed through the condo every time she screamed to be fed.

Grandma's delight over her new grandchild was a beautiful thing to see. She gushed and cooed over her, making observations on every little aspect of the child. I saw Christina every day, and though I agreed she was beautiful, I didn't really understand how people claimed to see any resemblance to a parent at that age – newborns had their own particular countenance.

"Mom," I said, in between bites of the scrumptious, tender sausage gravy that tasted every bit as good as I remembered. "Did I look like Dad when I was a baby too? You said El and Sophia did."

Mom looked up from her preoccupation of rattling the bright colored toys fastened to the handle of Christina's carrier. "What, dear?"

I swallowed another piece of biscuit. "You said Christina looks like Cole, but that we all looked like Dad when we were babies."

"Oh, yes. It's a funny thing. Girls seem to take after fathers, and boys favor their mothers. Most everyone I know says the same thing," she said, pouring herself a cup of tea.

Dad cleared his throat. "It's random," he said, his attention on his plate. "Just depends on which genes land where. There's no favoritism involved." He sopped up gravy with a chunk of roll and popped it into his mouth.

"You don't agree with Mom's theory?" El asked, reaching into the carrier and rearranging Christina's blankets.

Dad raised his head and looked at Mom while still chewing on his biscuit. His gaze switched to El, to Christina, and then to me. "Well, maybe you're right. You're all pretty good-looking," he said, cracking a smile.

El laughed. "Thanks, handsome."

Dad finished his meal and laid his napkin over his plate. "Great meal, wife. So, princess," he said, turning his attention to me. "Have you decided when you're coming home? Not sure I like the empty nest."

I toyed with my fork. "Um, I don't know, Dad. Still waiting to hear from Franklin for the winter admission."

He raised an eyebrow. "And if you don't?"

"There's lots of good schools right here." I tossed a glance at my sister. El smiled and gave a tiny nod of approval. "I might apply for one of them in the fall. Maybe even look into some of the top online grad programs. I'm really enjoying Rochester."

"And what will you do until then?"

I lifted a shoulder and let it fall. "Work, I guess. Save up some money."

He leaned his elbows on the table, interlacing the fingers of his oversized hands. "You could still come home. I know there's a young man there who's looking forward to seeing you again. You should get to know him better."

I ground my teeth and gripped my fork until my knuckles turned white. *Don't go there, Dad. Don't you want anything better for me than to be the Stepford wife of an ignorant bastard?* I glanced at the antique clock that hung in the adjoining living room. Ryder would be here in less than half an hour.

Setting down my fork, I drew in a huge breath. "Really? What a coincidence. There's a young man here in Rochester looking forward to seeing me, and I'm going to be late if I don't finish getting ready."

I excused myself from the table and started toward my room. "Hannah!" my mom called after me.

"Let her go," I heard my father say. "She's going to do what she wants anyway. Like always. Stubborn streak in that girl. Don't know where she gets it from."

"Gerry," Mom said in a hushed tone.

My mother's voice faded completely as I reached my room and closed the door. It was mostly my parent's room at the moment, their things laid out on the bureau and in the closet.

Stubborn?

Just because I didn't want to be married off to the first guy who showed an interest and had a steady job that *they* approved of? I felt like I didn't know my parents at all, the way they were behaving. Maybe having both my sisters 'taken care of' was making them put extra pressure on me. Did they have some crazy retirement plan I didn't know about?

I continued packing for my trip, sweeping any residual guilt aside and taking what I thought was most appropriate from the wardrobe I had on hand – sweaters, leggings, comfortable tees. But what would I sleep in? I owned a couple of nighties but mostly slept in pajama pants and tank tops. The thought of Ryder seeing me in any of it gave me chills of embarrassment.

As I stuffed one of each into the carry-on, I heard voices from the kitchen. Dad's, then Mom's. El must have gone to put Christina down for her nap. I couldn't make out any of the words. This was too weird. Mom and Dad didn't fight. I'd only heard them raise their voices to each other once before.

Closing my suitcase, I changed into what I planned to wear

while traveling. The sooner I left, the better by the sounds of things. I could wait for Ryder downstairs. The voices had quieted, so I opened the door and peeked out. My mom was clearing away the dishes, and my dad had settled in front of the TV. El and Christina had left the room.

"Well, I have to be going," I said cheerfully, setting my suitcase down by the hall closet and digging for my winter jacket with the faux fur trim. "I love you guys. I'll see you all in a couple days."

Mom turned to gape at me, probably hearing me for the first time that day. "It's the day after Christmas, Hannah Anne. Where are you going where you need to stay overnight?"

"Didn't Eloise tell you? I'm going skiing up at Lutsen Mountain. I've never been. I got invited kind of last minute." I shrugged on my coat and tugged the Sherpa hat over my ears. "I'll tell you all about my adventure when I get back." I picked up my suitcase and exited before anyone could say another word and spoil everything, especially my critical father.

CHAPTER TWENTY-FIVE

Ryder

"Thank you. You can reach me at this number." I ended my call with the Pulmonary Care Unit at the Mayo Clinic. I'd been told that my dad had experienced several severe respiratory episodes but had stabilized and would be moved to a co-op care unit a few blocks from the clinic within the week. Until then, he would remain in the ward for observation and treatment.

I felt like a shit for not going to see my father since the day after the fundraiser, but the old man himself had told me to stay away and focus on landing a contract with the Riot. There was nothing I could do for him anyway. But I had emailed my brothers, Braden and Colt, to let them know the situation but hadn't received a reply yet.

With everything going on around me filled with uncertainty, I couldn't wait to get out of town. Emotions and thoughts swirled inside my brain until I thought I might go berserk if I stuck around. My dad. The team. My job. Add to that the surprise ambush of Josée Thibault. Holy shit. When a woman said, 'I want to fuck you,' a man generally didn't ask questions, but I hadn't even been close to giving in. In fact, her actions had kind of disgusted me. After the shocking incident, I'd excused myself and left. A hookup like that was no longer what I wanted. With my thirtieth birthday knocking, it seemed I'd matured.

My phone pinged and I frowned as I recognized the number. Damn it all to hell. The incoming message put a damper on the semi I'd been harboring ever since the constant thoughts of Hannah naked and beneath me had consumed my rational mind.

Eloise Robertson Fiorino: Listen here. If you hurt my sister in any way, I'll cut your balls off with a dull knife. I know where you work, and I know where you live. This is the only warning you'll get. Heed it well, Martin. Never fuck with a hormonal and sleep-deprived woman.

After swiping the screen to erase the message, I rolled my eyes in frustration. Screw Eloise and her empty threats that didn't deserve a reply. If she was going to go after every man her baby sister dated, she was in for a world of frustration. But as for hurting Hannah, I'd never do that. Not intentionally. Hannah made my dark world as bright as any star in the night sky. I wanted to spend the next two days worshiping her, making her scream in pleasure, not pain. Hell, the way Eloise carried on you'd think Hannah was in high school not grad school.

It felt like a great time to disappear under the radar where no one would speculate on the status of my budding NHL career, and I had just the company to make the world fade away. As I packed my ski gear, I pictured Hannah again in a bikini and ski boots, wearing aviator shades as her auburn hair flew loose in the wind off a mountaintop like a curvier Lindsey Vonn. And even better, in a bikini in the hot tub at the lodge. Hell, without the bikini. My personal little snow bunny, unspoiled and untainted by any low-life douchebag to screw her over and leave her with a fucked-up view of men like her big sister. I often wondered who'd come before me to turn Eloise so bitter toward a man who'd just wanted to appreciate her softness. And I'd been speared for my trouble. Kind of like a dog nosing around after a fuzzy rabbit and encountering a prickly porcupine instead.

The thought of caressing Hannah's soft, sweet body as pristine as the hillside I planned to ski down made my cock press against my fly. So much for a semi. Despite Eloise and her smack talk, I'd now gone straight to full staff on the wings of my X-rated fantasies starring Hannah Robertson. And for once, they were about to come true. Throwing my bag in the back seat, I got into my car and pulled out of the underground parking, my tires squealing on the concrete. For a change, I'd have something to make my holiday vacation memorable.

CHAPTER TWENTY-SIX

Hannah

I looked down at the intimidating slope of white stretching before me. My knees already shook from my efforts to shuffle my way over to the bunny hill with what felt like two-by-fours glued to my feet. I must look even more ridiculous on skis than I had on skates. *Why in hell did I agree to this?* Panic and mortification filled my body in equal measure. *Because you're here with the hottest guy in Minnesota, and you're falling for him. You're focusing on yourself and what you want for the first time in a long time. Maybe ever.*

I'd be falling alright, of that I was certain. On my ski panted ass. But I had my handsome prince to pick me up again, if he didn't ditch me out of embarrassment before we even got to the lift. Ryder stepped into position beside me, his movements easy and graceful, the result of a lifetime of participating in outdoor sports. He looked out of place standing here on the kiddie hill, but he smiled just the same, melting a bit of my fear.

"I have to slide down... there?" I gulped, pointing ahead of me with my chin. I didn't dare free a hand from gripping the handles of my ski poles. After a few falls on my behind, I might be too sore for the other extracurricular activities planned for later. Darn and double darn. But I had to go now because the only way down the hill was on my skis or my butt.

Ryder laughed. "Yup. And later on, you'll have to slide down... there." He pointed his pole to the steep mountainside behind us.

I chanced a look over my shoulder. The panorama of the Lutsen Mountain ski area was beyond beautiful, a majestic vista of snow-covered peaks against a perfect azure sky, and it took my breath away. It had been hidden from view when we'd arrived, and I'd only seen the picturesque lodge iced with twinkling Christmas lights against a jagged snow-covered horizon.

"Oh, God," I said. Beautiful as it was, it didn't make me any less scared. Maybe we should have skipped the ski lesson for today and gone straight to the chalet. Or the bedroom. "I don't think so."

"Hey, it's easy. You're a quick study, look how you learned to skate in an afternoon."

"I had a good teacher."

"So you do, and he's not giving up on you." His dimpled smile made me feel like I could do anything, and I wanted desperately to please him. In everything.

"Okay, we'll start just like the kids do, with something they can relate to."

I blew out a breath. "What's that?"

"Food."

"Huh?"

"Pizza and French fries. Look," he said, moving his feet apart. "Put your skis parallel to each other, pointing straight ahead, like this." I gingerly lifted my feet to mimic his stance. "See, they're like two French fries side by side, right? When your skis are straight, you're going to go faster. Now, point your toes inward like this, and touch your knees together."

Again, I copied his movements, clumsily twisting my feet to angle the tips of the skis into a V shape. "Now you've made a shape like a pizza slice. When you want to go slower, you make a pizza. The edges of the ski will dig into the snow, like a plow.

Hence the term snowplow. But if I yell 'pizza' or 'French fry' it's easy to remember what to do – Pizza to go slow, French fry to go fast. Got it?"

"I guess so."

"Good. So make French fries, and I'll give you a little push to get started." I did as I was told, and Ryder's hand met the small of my back. With a steady push, I started moving forward down the slope. My skis made a swishing sound, and the slow glide was pleasant until I started slipping faster, then a little faster, getting farther away from Ryder as I went. A hoot of panic left my lips.

"Pizza," he called, and I remembered to point my toes and squeeze my knees together. I slowed immediately and then came to a dead stop. "Excellent," he said, gliding up beside me. "So just keep doing that until we get to the bottom, then we'll go up the lift to get a little higher and try again."

As I practiced these simple moves, I gained confidence, and we were soon riding the chairlift to mid-mountain. We played 'follow the leader' down the green runs, which I learned meant the easy, novice runs, just copying what Ryder did as he skied ahead of me, discovering that putting more weight on one side of the 'pizza' than the other would initiate a turn.

By early evening, I fell in love with skiing and wished I would have learned sooner. We stopped for an early dinner at the base lodge, sitting by a huge central fireplace with a massive copper dome and a chimney running up the height of the vaulted log-beamed ceiling. Whenever we'd gotten chilled throughout the day, we'd ski inside and enjoy spiked cider and mugs of mulled, spiced wine. Pine boughs and garland laced the entire place with holiday magic.

Around seven o'clock, we finally called it quits. Even though the ski area was flooded with light, allowing for skiing late into the evening, I didn't feel I was ready for that quite yet. "My legs are going to snap in half if I go down even one more run."

"Well, we can't have that, not with such pretty legs as those," Ryder said, pulling on the pompom of my hat. *Damn. If he turns up the charm dial any higher, the snow will melt right off this mountain.* "We can ski right down to our cabin door from here. Just take it slow and follow me."

We stacked our skis in a wooden rack on the porch of our cozy chalet unit, one of a dozen or so that were located at the edge of the hill across from the main lodge. I loved the rustic look of it, with its big log beams and posts and mullioned windows with white trim.

Inside was a sitting room with a stone fireplace, a bar and mini-kitchen and a bedroom with en suite bath. I showered while Ryder ordered dessert from the lodge dining room. We ate cheesecake and drank wine, and though I felt stiff and sore after such a physical day, I wouldn't have changed a thing.

Ryder picked up our wine glasses and led me to the big, wooden-framed sofa in front of the fireplace.

"This has been such a perfect day," I sighed as I sank into the soft cushions. My gaze tracked Ryder as he handed the glass to me and touched the rim with his own in a small toast. "Thank you for inviting me. It's the first time I've—"

"Been away with a man alone? I know. You're not that kind of girl — it's more than obvious. You don't have to explain yourself, I'm just glad you enjoyed it. You're a natural at winter sports. It's been my pleasure to coach you."

I smiled as I lost myself inside Ryder's amber brown gaze. He was so kind to me, so patient. I couldn't imagine how Eloise could say the things she did. I cared for this man, with an intensity of feeling I'd never known until now. The fire that crackled a soft, staccato rhythm in the background could just as well have been fireworks, proclaiming all the emotions I was feeling inside with blazing glory.

"A perfect day," I repeated. "Thank you."

A corner of his mouth turned up in a slow, sexy smile. "It's not over yet," he whispered, sliding his hand over mine as I rested it on the knee of his blue jeans. "In fact, the perfect part is just getting started."

I smiled back. What other surprises might Ryder Martin have for me to turn our ideal day into a satisfying evening? I'd almost forgotten it was the holidays. He hadn't yet given me a proper Christmas gift; leastways none with a shiny bow on top that I could unwrap. But this amazing trip, this dreamy chalet, and a picture-perfect day on the slopes was gift enough.

"It's not?" I asked innocently, wanting to hear the words come from his full lips – to know the depth of his desire for me.

He groaned deep and the grit in his voice tugged at my core. "I want to make love to you, Hannah. Please tell me you want that too."

I did. So, so much. The air between us shifted and heated, our breath mingling in the fire of the exchange.

He shook his head slowly, not breaking eye contact. I felt hypnotized, suspended in a happy bubble of bliss and excitement. I didn't regret leaving my family behind for the chance at a half price sweater or pair of boots. Ryder was everything I'd fantasized about in a man and couldn't imagine being anywhere else at this moment than here with him.

"We've got the whole evening ahead of us." He set our glasses down, then lifted my hand to his lips and kissed each of my knuckles in succession. "Just you and me."

"Our own little winter wonderland," I whispered, the words catching in my throat. I didn't think I could draw my next breath let alone say something worldly in this moment.

"All ours," he echoed, his eyes intense and searching mine. "Just like you're all mine."

A shiver ran down my spine, the power of his glance captivating and even frightening in a forbidden, delicious way. His dark lashes made a soft border around those passionate, beseeching eyes. He made light of our almost seven-year age difference, but I realized this was no college boy holding my hand and searing my soul with his scorching gaze, marking me as his. This was a grown man, his wants and desires unfamiliar to me. Would I be able to fulfill them? God, how I wanted to try. I trembled with uncertainty. Just the touch of his lips on my hand filled my stomach with a bevy of flittering butterflies. What would happen when they explored elsewhere?

Lower.

I felt as though I was standing at the edge of a deep pit, my body overcome with vertigo. The fall would be steep, merciless, with no hope of return if I gave in to what he wanted – what we both wanted. This night could change me. It *would* change me. This was a turning point in my life – a coming of age moment. The depth of the implications became such a wide expanse of turbulent emotion I might never climb out of it, if I even wanted to. Perhaps it was time to release control and fall.

Because Ryder would catch me.

"Hannah," he groaned, turning my hand so that he could kiss the pulsing underside of my wrist. "I want you." He pulled me toward him across the soft fabric of the couch we sat on in front of the fireplace. The acrid, musky smell of burning logs wafted around us, sweet, warm and tantalizing, like Ryder's luscious lips as they hovered near mine. "Now."

Our lips touched, only a whisper of contact to begin, then the crushing warmth of his mouth consumed me, wet and wanting and oh so sweet. I thought I might melt into its swelling need, the kiss like no other I'd ever experienced.

His hard, muscled body pressed against me, his hands seemingly everywhere at once. On my thighs, my behind and my breasts. My spinning thoughts coiled into panic. We were all alone now, not in a public skating rink within view of prying eyes. No one to see or hear, or to gossip, nor deter him from taking what he wanted.

But what did *I* want? I was infatuated with Ryder, had fallen for him hard, my ingenuous walls tumbling down like those of Jericho. I wanted to please him, give in to him, but I also wanted to be special to him, not just another hockey jock's conquest. Deep down I realized I really was behaving like a princess – holding out for Prince Charming and the fairy tale ending. Would my prince turn out to be the predator that El had railed against?

"Ryder," I gasped, prying my lips loose and clutching at his groping hands.

"What?" he murmured, repositioning his hands at my every attempt to repel them. His mouth moved to my throat, trailing kisses downward as his fingers unbuttoned my shirt. I gasped as he slipped my bra strap off my shoulder as well. His lips traveled farther south, across the exposed skin of my chest. The straining mounds tightened in response.

Everywhere he touched, I tingled and ached, making it hard to spit out the words that might send everything into an episode of crash and burn.

"I want you too," I breathed, "but... I need to know something."

Ryder froze, his seeking mouth just inches from my pebbled nipple. My heart throbbed, my chest rising and falling against his stubbled cheek. Neither of us spoke for a tortured minute, then Ryder raised his bowed head.

"What?"

"You're not seeing anyone else are you?" I tugged my lower lip between my teeth, feeling vulnerable and scared of his answer. I should have asked him the moment he invited me on this damn trip. "I... I've heard things about hockey players. I can't be with a man like this if he's seeing other people."

His eyes widened into moons. "Contrary to popular belief, my sweet Hannah, not everyone in the NHL is a manwhore. I'm not a monk – I have a past like any other thirty-year-old man. But I haven't seen anyone since I met you – even months before for that matter. You've consumed my every thought ever since I laid eyes on you at Casa Fiorino. Now stop thinking so much and just feel."

With that, his arms circled me, one hand slipping beneath my thighs. He rose from the couch, lifting me with him. "Ryder!" I shrieked. "What are you doing?"

"Making you mine. I can't wait one more second." His voice was a sexy growl. "Remember that night? The night of the fundraiser?"

"Yes," I croaked, hanging on for dear life.

"I've wanted to claim you ever since. And from the first time I heard your voice... I knew you belonged to me. Now, I'm going to prove it."

He strode to the bedroom with me slung in his arms like Scarlett O'Hara being taken up the grand staircase at Tara. Except instead of flailing my arms and legs, I clutched onto him with all my might, burying my face in his neck and inhaling deeply of his manly, intoxicating scent. After his searing admission and heartfelt words, I knew I wouldn't resist, whatever came next.

He laid me on the bed and caged my body with his own. Holding my chin inside the V of his thumb and forefinger, Ryder kissed me, his tongue insistent and forceful until my lips parted and allowed him entry.

His hand left my throat and resumed the work of undoing my buttons all the way and pushing my shirt aside. Clever fingers found the front clasp of my bra and popped it open like an expert. My aching core clenched with an unknown, powerful sensation at the same time his hand cupped my breast, squeezing and brushing his thumb across my nipple.

A helpless moan escaped my throat, finding no outlet as his seeking tongue scoured my mouth. My breasts swelled taut under the relentless touch of his thumb and sent a lightning bolt of heat through my core, causing a pool of slick wetness.

He released my lips, moving his body downward until his head lay against my chest, his thick sandy hair brushing my skin. "Hannah, you're so beautiful," he murmured, "so perfect."

His tongue reached out and laved my nipple in a slow, circling pass before taking it all in his mouth and sucking hard. I bucked upward, reaching. Searching. Every nerve screaming for more, as my nipple compressed into a hard, tingling nub inside the warmth of his mouth. My pussy throbbed, and as if in response, his fingers found the zipper of my jeans and pulled.

My breath came in excited pants, as my brain swirled in the maelstrom of impulses bombarding it. Ryder peeled my jeans away and his heated lips grazed my abdomen. "Ryder," I whimpered, no coherent words forming to express my feelings, or the uncontrollable sensations rocketing my body. "Ryder..."

He raised himself away from me. "Turn over," he urged, his voice low and rough. With a firm hand on my hip, he rolled me onto my stomach, my legs dangling over the edge of the bed. I could do nothing but gasp for breath and allow him to take control. Wanting to trust him, I surrendered to the moment. He stood and pulled the jeans down over the hump of my buttocks and down my legs until he could slip them off my feet. I heard the denim rustle and land in a heap on the wood-plank floor.

My panties followed, his fingers hooking into the filmy material and sliding them slowly, sensually past my cheeks and onto the floor. I waited face down on the soft comforter, the skin of my bare ass pricking into gooseflesh as I listened to the sound of his own jeans making an exit to the floor along with his shirt.

I felt his hands glide up the backs of my thighs, and I shivered, feeling another rush of moisture gather between my folds. *Please, Ryder, please touch me right now. Where I crave it.* He reached beneath my belly and slid me farther onto the bed, raising my hips upward and spreading my legs as he fit his body between them. He pulled what remained of my shirt and bra away and stroked my bare back with the palms of his hands, working his way lower and lower until they rested on the round globes of my behind. He circled them with his palms, then slid one hand around my front to spread the lips of my pussy that were now swollen with arousal.

I felt as though I would burst into flames, my body needing release from the onslaught of desire pulling at every muscle. He touched me there, at the very core of my slit, so precious and private where only he was allowed. Where only he'd ever been. His hardened cock pressed into the crease between my cheeks as his finger found my throbbing nub and stroked it, pulling a strangled moan from my lips.

At the first touch of a man's hands, I came undone. Dear God, I couldn't stop myself – a black wave of ecstasy overtook me and pulled me under like a relentless tide. As I rode high on the cresting wave, I writhed in sweet agony.

"That's it, baby, come hard for me." I heard Ryder's smooth

as silk voice croon from above. He kept stroking me through the thunderous seconds of orgasm that echoed through me before gradually receding. "Good girl," he whispered, his sexy smile showing through his words even though I couldn't see his face. I gasped for breath, limp, spent and overcome with emotion.

I felt him retreat from me, our bodies parting when the last thing I wanted was even an whisper of space between us. I heard the crinkle of a plastic package and realized he was putting on some protection. Safe sex was protocol, but in a way, I felt denied. I wanted all of him, all to myself, every raw, naked inch.

He rolled me onto my back, his chiseled torso poised over me. Muted beams from the lamps outside the curtained window outlined every curve and edge. He hooked his arm under one of my legs and pressed it upward, creating access for himself as he leaned forward and placed his hardness between my thighs, the tip of his sheathed cock pressing at my entrance.

"Hannah, I need you so bad," he whispered, "need to be inside you. I can't wait one more second."

The weight of his chest against mine, the pressure of his greedy, swollen dick, and his words caressing my cheek with wine-laced sweetness overwhelmed me. He was right. I belong to him, body and soul, with no option or desire to do anything but succumb to his claiming. I panted in and out, no verbal answer being necessary.

He thrust inside, my muscles resisting against a stinging pain. I gasped in shock – no one had ever said it would be this painful. This first time. Was I doing it wrong? God, I didn't want to disappoint him with my inexperience. Not this man who'd probably been with so many others. Fighting back the tears pricking my eyelids, I wrapped my arms around his corded neck and held on, bearing through it, trying to relax my lower body. The pain lessened as his steely rod penetrated my outer lips and thrust deeper, filling me. The short-lived burning became overwhelmed by a satisfying sensation of fullness. And possession. He moved within me, advancing and retreating, each stroke more forceful than the last.

His breath matched my own, raw and rapid. Tearful joy clenched my heart as I heard him speak, low and agonized. "So good, baby, so tight... God, you're beautiful..." I rocked in sync with him until his last powerful thrust, so intense that a tiny cry left my lips. "Hannah, it's been too long. Can't last..." Then he shuddered and stilled, his body quaking with his release.

"Ryder," I whispered, sniffing back joyful tears that refused to stay hidden behind my eyelids. I stroked his sweaty back and threaded my fingers through his tousled hair. His breathing slowed, and he raised his head and shoulders away from me.

"That was fantastic," he said, raising his finger to touch me on the nose, just as he'd done at the skating rink. His satiated smile faded as he looked into my eyes. "Uh-oh, what's wrong," he said, a hint of tease in his voice. "I didn't hurt you, did I?"

"In a good way," I whispered, still full of stampeding emotions.

He swiped away a teardrop that had escaped down the side of my face. "It's nothing to cry about. You're safe here with me. You said it yourself." He rolled off and laid on his back alongside me. I shivered as the cool air met with the veil of perspiration left behind on my chest and belly. He let out a relaxing sigh. "It'll be even better next time." I heard him peel off the condom and chuck it into the nearby trashcan. "If that's even possible."

His words sounded trite and the teeniest bit condescending, pouring a bit of ice water on the blazing heat between us. Did he not realize the importance of what we'd just done? Was that all he was going to say to me? Better luck next time?

"I thought the first time was pretty amazing," I said.

"Mmm," he grunted. "Yeah. The first time you're with someone you care about is pretty special."

"Or a first time with *anyone*."

Ryder seemed like he'd fallen asleep, he didn't respond. Then he snapped his head toward me. "What do you mean, with anyone?" he said, his words slow. "You mean first like, first ever?"

I bit my lip and grasped the edge of the comforter to at least partially cover myself. A chill swept my body as the moisture evaporated from my skin. "Yes," I whispered as fear strangled my tone. "Is that news to you?"

He exhaled and ran a hand through his hair. "Fucking A, Hannah. Why didn't you tell me? I would have gone slower. I would have been gentler with you. Shit, shit, shit. You're really not kidding?"

"Why would I kid you about that?" I said, becoming upset. "It's the truth."

He turned to me and raised up on one elbow. "I can't believe you're a virgin."

"No," I said hotly. "I *was* a virgin. Why are you getting angry?"

"I-I'm not angry," he stuttered, his face growing pale. "Just... you should have told me before. I feel like a complete asshole for not being more careful with you. I'm not the kind of dude who runs around deflowering virgins as a hobby."

"Why would I say something? It's not something you advertise. Would it have changed anything? Something wrong with being a... virgin?"

"No..." He shook his head, the look of disbelief still on his face. "I wouldn't have..."

"What? Wouldn't what? Asked me out? Kissed me? Made me feel like I was special?"

"You're doing it again," he said, pulling away, his face transforming into a cold mask. "And I have no idea why. Why is this becoming my fault? We can't even say it's a misunderstanding because I was the one who wasn't in the loop here."

My stomach flipped over and clenched tight. "Doing what? What am I doing? Expressing my feelings?"

"Acting like this. Like your first time has to be all white roses and fireworks and poetry. And it would have been... if you fucking would have given a man a heads up!"

I started to tremble, more tears threatening to spill over my cheeks. "I didn't ask for poetry, but I felt fireworks. Didn't you?"

He exhaled deeply and looked at me again before reaching up to stroke a strand of my hair, sliding its length through his fingers. "It was great, better than great. I like you a lot, Hannah, I do. This is new, and I'm not sure where it's headed and neither do you. But don't expect a royal proclamation over it."

I bristled. "I didn't ask for a lifetime commitment."

"You know I'm older than you. I can't say you're my first, but I'm not going to lay claim on you if I'm yours. That wouldn't be fair to either of us."

"I want you," I said past the emotion clogging my throat. "I gave myself to you, doesn't that make you happy?"

He let go of my hair and gently stroked the perimeter of my face with his fingertips, my cheek, my chin, my forehead. It felt sweet and soothing and intimate. "Of course it does. I just don't want you to think I owe you something I can't give you. At this point, I don't know what my future holds. All I can tell you is I love the way things are now and you're the only woman in my heart and mind. Let's not tempt fate by gazing into the crystal ball tonight."

You just don't want to see my face inside it, I thought bitterly. *I'm just another notch on the stick.* I rolled away from him and crawled under the covers, squeezing my eyes shut against the torrent of tears filled with shame over my own ignorance and regret over his reaction to taking my v-card.

CHAPTER TWENTY-SEVEN

Ryder

I brushed the snow that had fallen overnight off my windshield with slow, deliberate strokes. With every quick stroke, my mind drifted back to the night before. The best night of my life. And then I'd gone and blown it. Imploded the whole damn thing like an abandoned Vegas casino with my heartless words and icy cold attitude. I hadn't wanted to hurt her. I hadn't meant to push her away. She'd shocked the hell out of me with her admission. I'd never expected a woman of her age to still be pure. And then she'd gone and blamed me, sounding a whole lot like her uppity sister and the stress swirling my life had gotten to me. And I'd snapped.

Now, I didn't know how to act and what to say outside of a sincere apology. And I'd been doing that. Repeatedly. From the first kiss good morning, through breakfast and once again when we'd wheeled our bags to the car since we'd decided to leave a day early due to what had happened. I'd wanted to make love to her again – to go slow and make it perfect until she came all over my cock instead of my hand.

A do over. But she'd been so frosty I couldn't even thaw her out the tiniest bit, let alone touch her.

My feet and hands were already frozen, but the air outdoors was probably warmer than the atmosphere inside the car. Hannah sat silently in the passenger seat as the engine idled. She hadn't replied to any of my remorseful overtures with anything outside of a terse acknowledgement. Damn, I needed to crawl inside her head and figure out what she was thinking. I didn't know what else to say to her. She'd agreed to the trip, wanted to prove her independence. If she truly wanted a committed adult relationship, it started with open and honest communication. Yet when it came down to it, she was still a child in many ways, bolstered by her overprotective family.

Except one way. I'd taken her innocence. A gift I never expected to receive, and one I could never give back. What she wanted in return wasn't something I could offer, at least not until after the contract decision and after we got to know each other better. Only rash, immature people high on lust made lasting life decisions after a few weeks of knowing each other and one hot night.

Congrats, Martin. One more relationship in which you get to feel like a shithead. And a dirty old man. My days of wanting inexperienced girls had ended back in Juniors.

I opened the driver's door and got in, sliding the snowbrush behind my seat. "Hope the plows have been through," I muttered, wanting to say something. Anything to break the stilted and painful silence. "If the roads are bad, it might take a bit longer to get home." I chanced a look in Hannah's direction. She stared downward at her hands knotted together in her lap and nodded silently.

Shifting into drive, I pulled out of the lodge's parking lot. It would be a much longer trip if she wouldn't speak. I'd rather hear her say 'fuck you, asshole' than no words at all. For the moment, I'd leave her alone. She had to meet me halfway and she still refused to take even a baby step in my direction.

As we neared the halfway point between Duluth and Rochester, I needed to gas up. I pulled into an Exxon just off the highway. "You want anything, Hannah?" I asked as I grasped the door handle. "A drink? A snack?" Hannah shook her head, not meeting my gaze, her hands still clasped together as though to prevent herself from slugging me one in the mouth I'd put all over her perfect body. "Fine." I pulled the handle and stepped out. "There's restrooms in there if you need them." I pointed to the station's storefront, then closed the door against the chilly wind that had whipped along the stretch of open highway.

CHAPTER TWENTY-EIGHT

Hannah

Ryder twisted open the gas cap and inserted the fuel nozzle. He'd be a few minutes filling up, so I got out and dashed inside the station to find the ladies' room. I'd blown it and every pore in my body ached with shame and regret. Even my hair ached. When I'd agreed to date him – to go away with him, I'd thought I had my big girl panties on, but it turned out I was still wearing my Wonder Woman Underoos. I berated myself for not telling him when he'd first invited me to Lutsen. That way, he could have rejected me days ago and I wouldn't have to endure the excruciating humiliation of being rejected because I was a twenty-three-year-old virgin.

God, what must he think of me? A frigid, sheltered little girl who never strayed far from her mother's apron strings. Once inside, I grabbed my phone from my purse and dialed my sister. Not Eloise. That was one 'I told you so' I didn't need today. I felt sick to my stomach at what El would say about all of this. Because my heart... it felt like it was shattering into a million pieces.

"Hey, Hanna-bee. Merry Christmas! I called El's place yesterday, but they said you'd gone skiing. How was it? No broken bones, I hope?"

"Merry Christmas, Soph. No broken bones. Skiing was fun. I had a good teacher. I'll definitely do it again."

"Hmm, was his name Lars with an impossibly long Austrian surname and muscles big enough to carry you up the mountain without a chairlift? Like the Governator?" She faked a bad European accent, laughter in her voice.

Sophia's bright mood spawned a small grin on my face. God, I loved my sisters, even if one of them had acquired a Mother Superior complex right along with her new title as mother. "No, it's Ryder. I told you about him."

"Ohh, yes. The King of Kisses. He skis too? Man of many talents. Phil likes to ski when he can get away. Helps him think, he says, all that fresh mountain air. Frankly, I think he just likes the high he gets from the lack of oxygen."

I gave Sophia a weak chuckle. That mountain air seemed to make people reckless, as far as I was concerned. "Soph, I need some advice. I've only got a few minutes. When did you and Phil... you know... do it the first time?"

Sophia hesitated a moment. "You mean have sex? A few months after we started dating. I'd ask why you want to know, but I can guess."

I twirled a lock of hair between my fingers. "Did he treat you differently after that? I mean, did you guys know you were going to be together for the long haul?"

"Honey," Sophia said, heaving a sigh. "No one knows that. Sure, we were falling in love but look what happened. Even years later we had second thoughts, almost didn't get married. Just because you have sex doesn't mean you sign a contract. Sex is part of any healthy relationship, but not all relationships work out in the end. You can't put pressure on a man just to tie him down. He needs to be free to make his own decisions." She paused again. "Did you like it?"

I felt a blush rising despite my shame and regret. "Yes. It was... exquisite." It wasn't a lie. It felt amazing, mind blowing really. "But I felt awful afterward. He's had lots of women before me. But he's my first, and... he didn't seem to care. In fact, he seems really mad about it. Like I misled him because I didn't say anything beforehand. He wanted someone more experienced. I just know it. Even I've read *Fifty Shades*. I thought everything would come naturally like what you read about. I was wrong."

"Oh, sweetie, it does come naturally. You did use a condom, didn't you?" Sophia asked sternly.

"Well, duh. Of course. But he didn't know I was a – virgin." I spit the last word out like a piece of sour candy. "He acted like I withheld pertinent information, was trying to trick him or something. Like forcing him into marrying me." My voice cracked, and I sniffed back a tear. "I thought it made guys happy... to know they were the first, that they're special. I thought I was special to him, but now I just feel like another notch on his stick. I gave him the most precious gift I could... and it didn't mean anything to him. Maybe *I* don't mean anything to him."

"Hanna-bee, don't say that. You don't know what's going on in his head. He wouldn't have had sex with you and taken you away on a trip with him if he didn't have feelings for you. And you are special. Did he say he never wants to see you again? If he didn't, he just needs time to process. Sometimes when men are blindsided, they don't put their best foot forward. Between the stress of the holidays and the stress of his chance to make the Riot, he must feel like he's a French fry in a pressure cooker. He's probably never met a virgin before. There's not many of you left in this world, sadly."

"Well, there's one less, now." I started to cry aloud. "I think he wanted something... more. He wants someone better than me, Soph. Someone sexier."

"Listen," Sophia said, raising her voice to cut through my sobs. "Don't cry, sweetie. It's natural, it's normal. You did it responsibly and with someone you care about. Sex is meant to be fun too, you know. For both parties. It's like pizza. There's a million different kinds, but it's all pizza. And it's all good."

Why did she have to go and mention pizza? Flashbacks of skiing overtook my thoughts before sex ruined everything. Mind spinning, I laughed and sobbed at the same time. "Don't make jokes."

"There's only one way to find out what he's feeling. Ask him. Talk to him. If you can't be open with each other, then maybe you aren't right for each other. You can't say the wrong thing to the right man. At least you'll know where you stand, and you can stop tormenting yourself. I don't like knowing how upset you are, Hannah. Not after your first time. And I can't be there to hold you. It's breaking my heart."

I sniffed again. "Thanks, Soph. I gotta go."

I returned to the car to find Ryder sitting in the driver's seat drinking a Mountain Dew. As I got in, he offered me a Coke. "I didn't know what kind you liked."

"That's fine." I buckled up and took the bottle from him. "Thank you."

"You're welcome." He pulled out onto the highway.

I glanced sideways at him. With his jacket unzipped, his sterling chest and abs were clearly defined beneath a tight t-shirt. My hands itched to reach out and touch the chiseled indentations. His normally perfect hair sported a sexy bedhead tousle, and he wore dark glasses against the glare from the snow. He was still so gorgeous it hurt to look at him. I sighed with how much liked him. Maybe even more than that, if I understood what budding love felt like. I didn't want to lose him over some dim-witted, unrealistic fantasy I kept falling back into.

"I really enjoyed skiing," I said, choosing the safest topic for the conversation Sophia had suggested. "Thank you for teaching me and taking me on this trip."

He grinned but kept his eyes on the road. "You're welcome for that too."

The snowbanks on either side of the freeway shone with the light of the sun. "What are you going to do when we get back to Rochester?"

He lifted a shoulder, his face an expressionless mask. He wouldn't make this easy on me. And I didn't deserve it, not really. I could have opened the door after any one of his ten apologies that day, but I'd slammed it in his chiseled face each and every time. "I have a few days off. Just try to rest up and hit the gym a few times. Wait for the call."

My heart squeezed in my chest. For him. For me. For us. "You love hockey, don't you?"

The smile on his face looked almost sad somehow. "That would be an understatement."

"I hope you make the team then."

"Me too."

I looked away, staring out of the passenger window for a moment, focusing on my breathing and bolstering my courage for the elephant filling the car. The words that remained unsaid. The ones he was going to force from my lips. The landscape had changed from rocky highlands to rolling prairie as we traveled southward.

Once I'd calmed my racing heart, I continued in a small voice filled with every ounce of emotion I felt. "I liked having sex with you, Ryder. I can't pretend I didn't."

"That's good to hear," he said cautiously, and his hands tightened on the steering wheel, turning his knuckles into tiny white orbs. "I liked having sex with you too, even if it didn't conform to your expectations. Hannah, I *am* really sorry about how I acted last night. If I had it to do all over again, I'd..."

I flashed him a rueful smile and interrupted before I ruined another perfect apology. "It was wonderful, but I totally understand where you're coming from. So much is up in the air right now for both of us. I might not be staying in Rochester much longer. I expect I'll be going back to Columbus soon to start grad school. I've decided I'd like to get my Master's in accounting."

"I see," he said, his chest deflating with relief. He glanced at me and chuckled. "That'd be a little difficult then. Having more sex with each other. But I want to. Can we just agree to take it slow and fight the fire that's in front of us? Some of the things we humans worry about most have a way of working themselves out on their own."

Something fluttered in my stomach. Happiness over our truce and our understanding to take it slow. "Absolutely. But I still want to know everything about you. Have you always lived in Rochester?"

"Not always, but for a long time. I was born in Michigan."

"Is your family still there?"

"No. We're kinda spread out all over the place."

"My folks still live in Columbus. Where are your parents?"

"My mom passed away ten years ago. My brothers work in the oil industry overseas."

My heart ached with sadness for him. "Oh, I'm sorry. What about your dad?"

Ryder worked his jaw before answering. "We don't really get along."

"Huh. That's funny," I said. "Someone I know just said the same thing the other day. That he didn't get along with his three sons. That's so sad. Cole's mom said, 'parenting is a privilege, not a right.' Life's too short to be angry with each other, especially family.”

“Good advice,” Ryder said. “So you don’t want to be angry with me anymore?”

I thought of all the ways I could answer the question and decided on simply telling him the truth.

I blew out a long breath and turned to face him. “No. If I stay angry at you, I can never fall all the way for you. And I really want to. Even if it means we never see each other again. I want you to be my first broken heart too.”

He squeezed my hand and held it for the rest of the way to Rochester. Ryder dropped me off at the condo at around four o’clock. We shared a sweet kiss, but with no promises, given our uncertain immediate futures. When I got upstairs to the suite, no one was home. The Christmas tree lights were blinking white sparkles, and the living room and kitchen were in disarray. It seemed almost spooky.

As I dragged my case into the bedroom, my cell phone went off. It was my mother calling. “Mom, where are you? Where is everybody?”

“Oh, Hannah, are you home?” My mother’s frantic voice rose with panic and tore through the cell phone line. “I’ve been trying to get through to you, but it kept going straight to voicemail and service here is so spotty.”

“Just got in,” I said, heart dropping to my toes. “What’s going on?”

A pause. Too damn long of a pause. “Thank goodness. We’re all so scared.”

I could hear the emotion lacing my mother’s voice, shaky and high-pitched. It frightened me too, a light sheen of sweat breaking out on my forehead. “What’s wrong?”

“Little Christina started vomiting this morning, then broke into a fever. They think it’s something to do with her heart.

We're all back at the hospital in the NICU."

Stars dotted my vision. "I'm coming, Mom. I'll be right there."

CHAPTER TWENTY-NINE

Ryder

Dusk had dissolved into darkness by the time I got to my apartment. I felt tired after the long drive and emotionally drained. I didn't bother turning on any lights, just shuffled to my bedroom and flopped down. Fuck, everything in my life felt so messed up and uncertain right now. So many loose ends that I couldn't tie down, and it frustrated the hell out of me.

I'd hoped a couple days in the mountains would release all my anxiety, but it only created more. Though I had to admit to a certain amount of release while I was balls deep inside my precious Hannah, but this thing with her wound me up tighter than a torque wrench. I hadn't planned on making a lifetime commitment to the girl on the spot, just continue getting to know each other to see where it might lead. Clearly, she'd had aspirations for more than that, and I kicked myself for not recognizing it earlier. What had I been thinking, taking up with a twenty-three-year-old anyway? Because I'd just assumed she had college graduate experience? Fuck! What twenty-three-year-old didn't have at least half a dozen lovers past in this day and age?

Wrong move making assumptions, Martin. Now, my bad decision had come home to roost. All I needed was for Eloise to get wind of this and she'd be blowing up my phone with her dull knife threats.

I would just lay low for the next few days, blank everything out of my mind so that I'd be ready when the call from

McTaggart came. Either way, I could deal with it. If the answer was yes, I'd play for the Riot with every ounce of skill and heart I possessed. If the answer was no, well, I'd given it my all, and I had a great story to tell the grandkids. I closed my eyes and let myself drift off to sleep.

I didn't know how much time had passed when my cell phone shrilled in the pocket of the jacket that I hadn't taken off before collapsing into bed. I grabbed at it, still in a half-dream state. My voice came out thick and garbled. "This is Ryder."

"Mr. Martin, it's Louise Draper calling from the Pulmonary Care Unit. I'm afraid your father's taken a turn for the worse. His respiratory system seems to be shutting down. We're doing all we can, but I think you'll want to come to the hospital right away."

If I was still asleep, I must surely be having a nightmare.

"I'm on my way."

Once inside my Lexus, I hit my contacts for Braden. I didn't give a shit if it was the middle of the night over there. He could damn well get his ass out of bed and help me deal with this.

A sleep-drugged voice answered. "What the fuck, Ryder!"

I turned toward the hospital. "Screw you, Braden. It's an emergency. Did you think I would call you in the middle of the night just to check in?"

A pause and some rumbling around. "What's wrong."

"It's Dad."

My brother hissed a snort. "Did something happen in lock up? Old codger probably pissed off the wrong felon."

My fingers hugged the wheel in a vice grip. "He's been sprung for weeks. He's dying, bro. Lung disease from so many years on the job."

I imagined my brother trying to digest the information as I waited for a response that took a long time in coming. "Shit."

My stomach fell to my knees. "According to Mayo, he doesn't have much time left. You and Colt need to get on the next plane home if you want any chance of saying your goodbyes."

"Why should we get on a transatlantic flight just because the old man has decided he's going to leave this earth? Why should we even give a rat's ass?"

My mind raced because I knew where he was coming from. Dad had put us through the motherfucking ringer. How could I explain over the phone that I'd met an angel and she'd already made me a better man? A softer man? That pursuing my dream at my age had ignited a fire deep inside my soul that shone a bright light on the things that mattered most? That I now knew that if I let my dad die with words left unsaid between us that I'd regret it? I couldn't, but that wouldn't stop me from trying.

I sighed, deep and long. "I'm sure you probably won't believe me, but he's changed since he got the news. He's never going to win any father of the year awards, but I think if you don't come home, you'll be sorry. There are words that need to be said between the two of you. Colt too."

"I'm not sure I care, but I'll talk to Colt and let you know."

"I guess that's all I can ask."

CHAPTER THIRTY

Hannah

The green vinyl armchairs in the waiting room outside the NICU unit hadn't gotten any more comfortable with the passage of several hours. I shifted my bum again. Not that it felt any better, but at least any bruising would be even on both sides. I looked over at Mom, her distress having given way to exhaustion as she slumped limply in her chair. Dad sat nearby, his legs stretched out and his head back, snoring lightly.

I could barely bring myself to look at Eloise. My big sister, the strongest person I'd ever known lay curled up in her husband's arms, looking frail and fetal, her expressive eyes red-rimmed and sunken. How could I have ever felt any animosity toward any of these people around me? My family? The only family I had. Life was too short. And that fact was driven home all too keenly when the tiniest member of that family struggled for hers at only a few weeks of age inside a surgical room.

It was not uncommon for premature babies to have underdeveloped organs, and we'd been told a small repair to one of Christina's heart valves was routine and would fix the problem permanently and without complications. But it did not assuage the pain and worry we all felt.

I got up and went to sit in the chair next to my mother. She started, then smiled and put her hand on my arm. "Almost dozed off there," she whispered.

"You're allowed, Mom. Rest while you can."

"Did you have a nice time skiing? You left in such a hurry,

and so early in the morning. Why, I didn't even get a chance to hug my baby daughter and wish her safe travels."

"Yes, it was fun. I'm sorry I missed shopping with you guys. How was it?"

"Oh, it was wonderful. Theresa came with us and then she made the most delicious dinner for all of us ladies. It certainly helps to have a restaurant owner in the family. Theresa is such an incredible cook and hostess. I'd never admit it in front of your father, but it was so nice to hand over the reins for once and be served by someone else."

"I suppose so," Hannah agreed. "You know, I did leave in a hurry. I was so excited to go skiing. I'm sorry I have such a 'stubborn streak,' as Dad said. Don't know where I get it from."

Mom looked into my eyes, a warm twinkle glowing there. "From your dad, of course," she said, a smile playing at the corners of her mouth. "Don't you know that's why you two can sometimes be at odds with each other? You're so much alike."

I snickered. "You're right. He doesn't even think he's stubborn. He just maintains his way is better."

"Wha...?" Dad snorted, waking up from his nap.

"Nothing, dear," Mom soothed.

All eyes snapped up as the surgeon entered the room. "Mr. and Mrs. Fiorino?" Cole stood, folding Eloise into his embrace as he did so. "Christina's doing great. The procedure went exceptionally well, no worries at all. She should grow up to be a strong and healthy girl with no heart issues whatsoever. Provided she eats right and exercises, of course."

A collective sigh of relief echoed in the room. "When can we see her?" El asked.

"She'll be in recovery for a while. You might want to go home for the night."

"No," El said immediately. "We'll stay."

"Now who's the stubborn one," I whispered to my mom.

"The rest of us should get some shut-eye," my dad said. "I'll take these ladies home, if you want to stay, Eloise."

"That's probably best since you have flights to catch tomorrow."

"Alright, ladies, if you please?" he gestured us to the exit.

"I'm going to call Sophia and let her know everything's alright," I said. "And I want to stop in on another patient before I go."

Mom patted my arm. "We'll wait."

I walked over to El and wrapped both her and Cole in a hug. "I'm so glad everything's okay. I'm sorry we argued, El. I've learned so much from you, thank you for being my big sister."

"You came back in one piece," El said, a wan smile crossing her tired face. "You must have taken at least some of my advice."

Nodding, I broke away and walked down the corridor to make my phone call. Sophia answered, and I gave her the update on the situation. "Thank goodness Christina will be fine," Sophia said. "How are you doing? Better than the last time we talked?"

"I'm good. I'd tell you the whole story, but at this point, I'm not sure how it's going to go. You'll be the first to know when I find out."

"I'll hold you to that."

"By the way, I meant to ask you. Mom and Dad had a fight in El's kitchen, right before I left. I've never heard them argue like that, not since that night you ran off in the woods."

"What was it about?"

"I don't know. It started over Russ, believe it or not. Dad still has it in his head that I'm going to come home, marry the man and live not happily ever after. I got mad and left the room, but

I heard Dad say I have a stubborn streak and wonders where I got it from, and then Mom tells him to be quiet, and then I couldn't hear the rest. But they were loud."

"Oh boy."

"What did they fight about that time, Soph? Maybe it's the same old argument."

Sophia sighed audibly, the air causing my phone to crackle in my ear. "Hannah, El and I swore we'd never tell you this. I can't believe you even remember that night, but since you obviously do, maybe your knowing can help Mom and Dad put it behind them once and for all."

I stuttered to a stop, Sophia's words somehow filling me with dread. "Tell me what?"

"Mom had an affair. A long time ago, with one of Dad's co-workers."

I gasped, my hand fluttering to my throat. "No. I don't believe it."

"There's more. Mom got pregnant, and after you were born, Dad found out about her and Jack, that was his name. They were going out to a company party, and they started arguing about Jack, and the fact that... oh, Hannah, I'm sorry... that Jack might be your natural father."

I swallowed hard but couldn't get the lump to go down. It was unthinkable, but the pieces started to fit. I looked different than my sisters. I'd come along much later than El and Soph. And what Mom had said just now, about being stubborn like my dad. "How do you know all this? And why wouldn't they just get a DNA test?" I asked, my voice shaky.

"I overheard their whole conversation. I was behind the drapes, playing hide and seek with El. They didn't know I was there. When I came out, I asked them if it was true. I got upset and ran out. You know the rest."

I leaned against the wall, almost dizzy, whether from this news, or the exhausting day, or both. "Holy shit."

"That's a lot to take in, I know. But look, you're my sister in every way that matters, and I love you. Mom and Dad love you, no matter what."

"Love you too, Soph," I said in a voice that was so low I could barely hear it myself. Footsteps approached and I shook my head, giving myself a mental shake. "I'd better go. Bye."

I turned to see my folks walking toward me. "Hannah, are you alright? We've called a cab, it'll be here in a minute."

I had difficulty looking at my parents as I desperately tried to absorb everything I'd just learned. "Oh, yeah, uh... you guys go on without me. I still have someone I want to visit. I'll get home on my own, don't worry. I'm not that tired."

My mom clucked her tongue, narrowing her eyes. "You sure? You look a little pale."

I forced a bright smile. "Positive. I'm fine. See you at home."

I turned and nearly sprinted down the corridor. I needed time and space to think. I didn't expect the old man from the restaurant to still be at the outpatient clinic, but it was an excuse to put some distance between me and my parents right now.

After searching out the nurse's station in the Pulmonary Care Unit, I asked if a patient named Walter happened to be there. "Last name?" the nurse asked.

"I actually don't know it. He's an elderly man, with a rough voice, bushy gray hair?"

"Oh, that Walter. Yes, he's here, but he's already got a visitor." The nurse looked around, then leaned forward and lowered her voice. "I shouldn't be telling you this, but the poor man rarely has a visitor and..."

I was familiar with all of the privacy rules and gave the nurse a friendly smile. "I promise not to tell. Me and Walter are old friends."

The nurse looked up and down the hall again. "Well, he's been very sick. Seeing a friendly face might help. Room E-510, down this way."

"Thanks." My shoulders sagged. This was a sad way to end a day that already had its share of sadness.

I walked slowly to room E-510, not knowing what I might see. I peeked in the door, a semi-private room with the privacy drapes pulled around the far bed by the window. The other bed lay empty. I walked in and saw a pair of legs sitting in a visitor's chair behind the drape.

"Walter?"

The visitor stood up and swung the drape partly away to see me and I stopped dead in my tracks. Ryder stood there, looking as stunned as me.

"Hannah?" His velvety voice was pared down to a hoarse whisper. "What are you doing here?"

"I came to see Walter," I said, stepping closer. "You know him too?" I reached for the edge of the drape and pulled it toward me, enough to see around to the bed. "There you are." I struggled to keep my voice normal. "How are you today?"

Walter couldn't speak with the ventilator tubes inside his throat. A machine huffed and puffed on a stand next to the bed, connected to the tubes. He looked terrible but managed to raise his arm a bit to acknowledge my greeting. I nodded, then looked to Ryder, my eyes speaking the questions that my mouth would not.

He inhaled a shuddering breath. "Hannah Robertson, this is my father, Walter Martin. Dad, this is my... girlfriend. Hannah."

Girlfriend? Hearing the word was as joyful to me as the

scene before me was bitter. I was going to cry again, for a whole bunch of new reasons. I gave a small wave and then leaned over to squeeze Walter's hand. He reached up and cupped my cheek with his weathered hand. "Hi, Walter. Good to see you again. I'll let you two spend more time together," I said, backing away from the curve of drape. "I didn't mean to intrude."

"Wait in the hallway?" he asked, a pained expression on his handsome face. "I want to explain."

I nodded and pivoted away, hiding my own wretched expression. This night had gone beyond all explanation. As I waited in the hallway, I wrapped my arms around myself. In a minute, Ryder stepped beside me and leaned against the wall with his hands in his pockets. "So, I know you've met my dad before. I saw you help him at Casa Fiorino. Seems you made quite an impression on him with your sweetness."

I met his gaze. "Why weren't *you* helping him?"

"Because I didn't know he was there until I saw you with him. He wasn't invited."

I threw my hands up between us. "So? You should have come running."

"You don't understand." Ryder's expression spoke of his guilt as he tried in vain to explain. I'd never had experience with family that didn't love me. What he was saying made me struggle to comprehend. "He's a miserable drunk who treated me and my brothers like shit for years. He fucked up on the job and was sent to prison for criminal negligence in the death of a co-worker. He just got out right before the charity event and tells me he has a terminal lung disease, and here we are. The softness he shows to you is a new character trait for the man. End of story."

My kind heart squeezed inside my chest. "And all that means he doesn't deserve your help? He's still your father. You knew

I'd met him, and you didn't say a word the whole time we were seeing each other? You were that ashamed of him? That cruel?"

Ryder turned on me. "Damn right I'm ashamed. What did I just hear earlier today, uh, 'parenting is a privilege, not a right?' Well, he lost all his privileges when he smacked us around, berated us, and loved a whiskey bottle better than any of us. He especially lost his privileges when his drunken ass *killed* a man, leaving that man's little kids without a father they adored!"

I went silent, suddenly understanding his pain, and my own, and that we were more similar than different. I was judging him again and not walking a mile in his shoes. Perhaps there was more of Eloise inside me than I'd ever realized. I leaned against the wall next to him. "I didn't come here just to see Walter," I murmured. "El's baby was rushed here for emergency heart surgery this afternoon. It was so scary and she's so little. I didn't find out until I got home. I was having sex while..."

"Oh, Jesus, Hannah... I..." He shook his head, no other words coming out.

I fell into his warm embrace as the first tears fell. "She's okay. She's going to be fine. Ironically, I found out something about my father too. That he might not be my real father. But for twenty-three years, he didn't complain. He didn't shun me. He was a father in every other sense of the word. He loved me anyway. So yeah, it is a privilege. I'm sorry that Walter didn't see it that way. You deserved better, Ryder."

"I'm tired," Ryder said after a moment. "Are you?"

"Bagged is more like it."

"Would you like to come home with me? I'm sure it's less crowded than at your sister's. Please give me a chance to make Lutsen up to you, and to take away some of your pain. Mostly the portion that I've caused."

I gestured toward the room behind us. "What about Walter?"

"He's stable right now, and the nurses said they'd call me if he takes another turn for the worse. Besides, I've said my goodbyes, and so has my dad. We've forgiven each other. There's been closure and now there's peace."

I drew in a big breath. I really was tired. Exhausted. "Well, if you promise to come back here and be with him if they call. And since I'm apparently your girlfriend now..." I said slowly a small smile playing on my lips. "I suppose I have privileges too."

"Damn straight." He reached for my hand, and I clasped it firmly. "Let's go, sweet girl."

CHAPTER THIRTY-ONE

Ryder

My palms were sweaty as I once again lingered in the reception area outside Shane McTaggart's office. I couldn't tell from Shane's tone of voice on the phone whether he had good news or bad. If it was bad, I'd likely be spending New Year's Eve alone with a bottle of Murphy's Finest, re-thinking my life. Even Hannah wouldn't be able to love that pain away. If it was good, well. It was very, very good.

Always the early bird, I still had fifteen minutes until my scheduled appointment. Time for a quick call to Hannah for fortification. Dad's death had thrown me for a loop and with the Riot's decision pending, a maelstrom of turbulent emotions had bubbled to the surface, refusing to be tamped down by my usual defense mechanisms.

"Hi, sweet girl," I cooed into the iPhone before she could speak.

"Hi, yourself. Aren't you supposed to be in a very important contract negotiation?"

I chuckled. God, I loved the way she always put me right at ease. Made my life so much better. So much brighter. "I like the way you think. Thanks for the vote of confidence but I'm still sitting in the lobby. I'm not going to check in with reception until it's time. Important to collect myself and all that. First, I need to talk to you about something. I was up all night and it wasn't just because of the Riot."

A pause and I could almost see her pulling that full bottom lip between her teeth. "Oh?"

"I'm having mixed feelings about my dad," I said on a deep sigh. "I'm not sure I did the best that I could where he was concerned. You know... at the end. I was so damn focused on making the team I kind of let everything else important fall to the wayside."

"You did the best you could, Ryder," Hannah said, empathy oozing from her soft voice. Ever since we'd returned from our weekend together, Hannah had become my best friend. After seeing her handle a painful life experience, I'd been so impressed. I was so falling in love with this incredible woman – the first person to ever fully support me. Hannah was my number one fan and I could count on her as surely as I could my next breath. "Your relationship with Walter was complicated. He wasn't there for you as a father, not until the bitter end. It's normal to have conflicting feelings about him leaving prison just to have him die. But think about the good times. You've told me some heartwarming stories about what a great dad he was before the demons of addiction overtook his good sense. And your last conversation with him went well. You were also able to get your brothers to come home and say their goodbyes to Walter. That should give you some peace of mind."

I wished I could reach through the phone and pull her toward me for a searing kiss of gratitude. "You're right. As always. Hannah, I want you to know how much I appreciate your wise counsel. It's nice to have someone who has normal family values and experiences to use as a sounding board. I may just have to keep you."

She laughed, the tinkling sound like music to my stressed-out ears. "Hmm... I'll have to decide whether or not I want to let you. Now, go get 'em before McTaggart gives you a delay of game penalty."

After saying goodbye, I nodded to Joyce, Shane's personal

assistant and waited until she pushed a few buttons on her office phone.

"Shane and Lou are ready to see you now, Mr. Martin," Joyce said.

The door to the office opened, and Shane stuck his head out. "Come in, Ryder."

I swallowed and forced my feet over the threshold. Across from Shane's desk sat the Riot's GM, Lou Spieker.

"I believe you know Lou," Shane said.

Lou nodded. "Ryder."

Shane seated himself behind his desk. "Since it's New Year's Eve and I'm sure we're all anxious to start the celebrations early, I'll cut to the chase. Ryder, as you know, the players selected from the open tryouts were not guaranteed a contract, nor would they necessarily be offered a contract from the team they tried out with."

I nodded, nerves twisting my guts into an intestinal pretzel. "Yes, that was my understanding."

"Right. And as you know, we have to consider the best interests of both the team and the players. Lou?"

My head swiveled to face the man.

Lou smiled and nodded. "We liked what we saw, Ryder. We think you're a great fit for our defensive squad and are prepared to offer you a signing bonus in addition to a competitive salary."

I blinked and glanced from Shane and back to Lou. "You're offering me a position on the team?" I asked, looking for confirmation that I understood them correctly. "A contract?"

"Yes," Shane chuckled. "We expect you'll want to look over the numbers before giving us an answer of course, but we think you'll be pleased with the offer."

As my heart flipped over and squeezed, my mouth went as

dry as the Sahara. I couldn't speak past the lump of emotion in my throat. My dream had just come true. The motherfucking NHL!

So why was Hannah the only thing I could think about?

CHAPTER THIRTY-TWO

Hannah

My hands shook as I held the envelopes that El had brought from the mailbox downstairs. I stared at them as I stood amid packing boxes in preparation for the Fiorino's move to their new house in Scenic Acres.

One bore the imprint of Franklin University, Columbus, Ohio, and inside, it held the decision that would change my life forever. Or at least the next few years. The other was from Mayo Health Sciences.

Which would hold the ticket to my future? One? Both? Neither?

"Are you going to open them or frame them?" El nearly shouted. "The suspense is killing me, little sister."

I sliced the Franklin envelop open with a fancy opener from El's desk. The paper inside felt thick and weighty. Official. I unfolded and read it, taking my time. Then I opened the second one, doing the same.

"Well, that's that," I said, folding the letters up again.

"What? Let me see that," El scolded, reaching for the letters. I handed them over. El opened one then the other, scanning them intently. Her eyebrows knotted in concern. "What the hell is this?"

"I'd better tell Ryder," I said with a sigh.

"Will it matter?" El asked, looking at the letters again.

I shrugged. "I hope so. I'm meeting him at the restaurant in an hour, before my shift starts. I should get ready."

It began to snow again as I reached the entrance to Casa Fiorino. The neighborhood still sparkled with Christmas lights, and the area businesses had joined together in creating a public outdoor square to host New Year's festivities tonight. Volunteers moved about, stringing up shiny fringed banners and tall poles with lighted shapes at the tops, and erecting a small stage for performers. Fireworks would be set off on the rooftops of the higher buildings surrounding the square at midnight.

The New Year beckoned with the same exciting sizzle and flame of the planned celebrations. A time for new hopes, new beginnings, and new plans, and I hoped for all the above in what lay ahead for me.

For Ryder, all of that hung on the outcome of his meeting with the coach this morning. After leaving the hospital, we'd spent the night together in his apartment, sharing our hopes and dreams and fears. His brothers had arrived the next day, so I'd left him to reconnect with them and deal with the inevitable outcome of Walter's condition. That was what families did, share the load and be kind to each other because you never knew how much time you had left.

When Walter died the day after his other sons arrived, I'd supported Ryder through the funeral. It was heartbreaking to see such a strong, alpha male cry, but I took solace in the fact that Ryder and Walter had come to terms with their relationship at the end. Nothing had been left unsaid.

Regarding my own family, I'd decided not to confront my parents about my paternity. Why put them through such a thing when nothing would ever change about how I felt for them both? I just didn't have it in me to break my father's heart — not when my mother's indiscretion had already wounded the strong, tough man. And not right after I'd witnessed the familial conflict in Ryder's life and the lingering aftermath.

I chose a table for two near the windows, so I could watch for him and enjoy the activity going on in the square while I waited. Through the accumulating snow, I soon recognized his strong, athletic frame as he approached the building, and then slipped inside. I waved to him, and as he walked toward me, I could practically feel the anxiety and excitement emanating from him.

I stood and held my hands out to him. He took them in his, the skin on his gloveless palms cold to my touch. "How'd it go?" I asked, my gaze seeking his. "Are you okay?"

"Yeah. We better sit down," he said, sounding breathless as if he'd ran the whole way from the arena. We sat across from each other, hands still intertwined on the tabletop.

"I got my letters today," I blurted, "but I want to hear your news first."

"No, you go first," he said. "I'm still trying to wrap my head around mine."

"I got accepted," I said, a bittersweet smile forming on my lips. "To Ohio." I released Ryder's hands to get the letter from my purse and showed it to him. "Read it."

He sniffed inward as he spread the letter out in front of him, his nose starting to run from his walk in the cold. "You changed programs..." he said, his eyes scanning back and forth, then looked up in surprise. "Nursing? You're going to be a nurse?"

I nodded. "I got the idea after hanging around Mayo so much. I discovered I liked helping people, people who need it. Turns out I had better grades in all the prerequisites than I did for the accounting program."

"That's..." he looked down at the paper and then met my eyes again, "great. I wish you all the luck in the world. And I'm never going to forget what you were to my dad. He couldn't stop talking about his pretty angel girl and how much he adored her. You made his last days better. For that, I'm forever grateful. He and I didn't have the best relationship, but at least we were able to connect at the end. It's something…"

"Thanks, but there's more." I pulled out the other envelop. "I also applied to the nursing school at Mayo, and I was accepted. Now I just have to decide which one I want to attend."

A smile spread over Ryder's lips. "I know which one *I* want you to attend."

My heart squeezed and a tear slid down my cheek. "Enough about me. Tell me about your meeting."

The smile grew even brighter as he leaned forward and took both of my hands in his. "They want me, Hannah. They're making me an offer. I still can't believe it."

I squealed and brought his hands up to my lips, kissing his knuckles. "I knew they'd make you an offer. They'd have been stupid not to." I beamed at him, my heart overflowing with joy. For both of us. "Congratulations on fulfilling your dream."

A grin formed on his fresh-shaven face that blossomed into his signature, full-on pearly smile. It felt like sunshine, melting away the ice and snow and drying the waterworks that sprung from my eyes. I could barely focus on his actual words.

"Well, call it a dream or a fairy tale, take your pick. It still feels unreal to me. They offered me a signing bonus on top of a salary. I'm a Riot. Will you be a Riot with me? Two Riots have to be better than one."

My heart seemed to swell and take up space in my throat as well as my chest. It beat a joyful rhythm that would not be contained. I jumped from my chair and flew into his arms. He caught me and framed my face with his hockey-playing hands to deliver a kiss that consumed us both.

It was both a dream and a fairytale, I knew, but one based in reality. My prince really had walked through the door to rescue the princess and take me away. To a place where neither towers nor ice castles would stand in the way of our happy future together.

CHAPTER THIRTY-THREE

Ryder

"I can't believe you're doing the girlfriend thing, Martin," Jones said, stabbing me in the gut with his pointy elbow. "Although, she is a total smokeshow."

I followed his gaze with my own to land on my girl and my heart squeezed in my chest. "You're not getting any younger, Jones. You might want to consider slowing the hell down before you end up with something you have to carry around like luggage. And not nearly as nice as Louis Vuitton."

My friend scoffed and scrubbed a hand down his beard growth. "That never happens. Not if you wrap it."

I snorted a laugh. "You're going to get sick of meaningless sex, you know. I did."

"Well, maybe if a chick comes along that's as hot and sweet as your Hannah, I'll change my mind. But until that time…"

Jones waggled his eyebrows and wandered off toward a circle of puck bunnies standing near the bar at Casa Fiorino waiting for his autograph. On their tits.

I glanced around the restaurant from the streamers and balloons, to the champagne fountain and hot hors d'oeuvres buffet all courtesy of Hannah's stellar planning skills. With a little help from Spud.

As I gripped my craft beer, my heart felt full. When Eloise and Cole had offered to throw me a celebratory party in honor of my NHL contract as an olive branch, I'd grabbed it with both hands. Since motherhood, Eloise seemed to have softened a bit, her daughter making her the best version of herself. A version I almost didn't recognize.

Since she wasn't threatening to castrate me anymore, I'd even started to like her.

Just a little bit.

Warm arms snaked around my waist, tightening my crotch. "Do you like your party, my hunky NHL man?"

I put my hands over hers and squeezed. "Yeah, but I think I'm going to like the after party even more. Can you think of any special ways to party plan our alone time?"

She leaned up and nipped me on my ear, whispering. "How about another first to mark this occasion?"

My ears perked up along with every other part of my body. "I'm all ears."

Hannah nuzzled her face into my neck. "I want to put my mouth all over you."

Damn. My life. My woman. Everything had fallen into place for a fuck up like me. I still couldn't believe it. I spun in her arms and placed a sweet kiss on her lips that didn't match the rawness of the conversation. "You need to stop or I'm going to be sporting a rod at my own event. If Jones sees it, I'll never hear the end of it."

She smiled, those full lips splitting her face wide. "Don't you like it? It's my new naughty side."

"If your sister wasn't glaring daggers at us, I'd put your hand between my legs and show you how much I like it. After you put your mouth on me, how about I get to spank your sexy ass like I've been wanting to since I first saw it in that pink silky dress right in this very spot."

Her eyes widened into moons. "Like hard?"

I bussed a kiss to the top of her head and gave her perfect rump a little squeeze despite El's stink eye. "Only as hard as you want. I know you well enough by now, Hannah. I'd never try anything with you I didn't think you'd like. Do you trust me?"

That smile could blind a man. "I trust you. So it's a date? For later? For sucking and... spanking."

I winked at her as my balls tightened to an uncomfortable ache. I took another swig of my beer, so I didn't carry her out of here right now, caveman style. "I wouldn't miss it. If I forget to tell you, later is my favorite part of this evening. Even more than my kick ass new contract. More than this kick ass party you threw in my honor. Because later belongs to just me and you."

She blew me a kiss over her shoulder as she sashayed away, knowing what seeing her behind would do to me. Cheeky wench.

Cole and Shredder wandered over, Cole screwing the top off a bottle of beer. "So, does your fancy new contract mean we have to like you now?"

I shook Shredder's huge hand and he said, "Since he's the D and protecting both our asses, I suggest you start being a little nicer, Fiorino."

Kylie walked up behind Shredder and hugged his waist. She seemed so tiny next to the huge goalie. She tossed me a saucy wink that sent her pink hair bouncing. "Way to go, Ryder Martin. I'm duly impressed and so, so happy for you!"

Cole nearly choked on his swig of beer. "Let's not get carried away, Politskis. He's not our only defenseman."

I raised one eyebrow. "But I'm the best one."

Cole picked at the label of his beer bottle. "Confident, aren't we? I like that, Martin. Keep it up and keep your head up on the ice, so you can feed me the puck. You might be our offensive minded D-man, but I'm actually paid to score goals and a lot of them."

Eloise arrived holding Christina, and Cole leaned over his baby with love oozing out his eyeballs. And then he cooed. He fucking cooed to a baby in a bar.

"Congrats, Ryder. I know you're going to do great this season." After handing Cole little Christina, she reached out and touched my shoulder, and I didn't recoil. "It's so amazing that you were given a second chance at your dream. Would you like to hold Christina?"

Cole snatched the baby closer to his chest. "No can do, PDL. The ink might not even be dry on his new contract, but his hands aren't *that* good."

I shook my head, wrapping my fingers tighter around my beer. "Nah, I'm good. Besides, I've been drinking. Maybe he shouldn't even be holding the baby, El."

From across the room, Hannah gave me a lingering look, tugging her lower lip between her teeth which she knew drove me to distraction. I finished off my bottle and said my thank yous and goodbyes to the Fiorinos and the Politskis.

"Think it's time for me and Hannah to head home," I said, surprised when El grabbed me in a hug.

"Take care of her, okay?" she whispered in my ear.

I hugged her back with everything I had, forgiving and forgetting anything and everything in our past. "I plan on it. You don't have to worry, El."

She looked me up and down and seemed to accept my words for once instead of arguing with me. "Actually, I'm okay with this now. You've proven yourself so far. Just don't blow it. Hannah's worth it, Ryder. She's worth everything."

Smiling, I turned to walk away and find my naughty girl so we could go home and start our sucking and spanking session. My entire body tightened at the thought.

I'd only drifted a few feet away when I heard Cole call out. "Hey, Martin!"

I glanced over my shoulder and saw him standing there cradling his infant daughter in his huge arms. She looked like a tiny baby doll wrapped in pale pink with fragile limbs, perfect, porcelain skin, shocks of black hair the mirror image of his, and a tiny bow on her head. "Yeah?"

"Welcome to the team. More importantly, welcome to the family. And if you hurt my favorite sister-in-law, it's gonna be you and me, your balls and a dull knife. Capisce?"

Despite his threat, my lips tugged upward. They no longer meant anything because just like my former frenemy Fiorino, I had *everything.* "Got it."

EPILOGUE

Hannah

One year later...

"This time, we're doing it right, sweet angel. Just like my NHL career, it's a do-over. Our own personal rebound. Like when a lightning fast one-timer gets shot from the point and resumes another life straight into the net."

I snaked my arms around Ryder's neck, snuggling into the warm skin of his throat, my deep inhales picking up hints of a woodsy cologne and man.

My man.

His booted foot kicked in the doorway, and he carried me over the threshold as if I weighed nothing.

His lips brushed my cheek. "Your house, madam."

I lifted my head from the safety of his arms only long enough to glance around the home Ryder had purchased with his savings bolstered by his signing bonus. We'd decided to create a permanent space for ourselves in Rochester, only a short hop from the arena. Close enough that I could visit El and Christina anytime I wanted.

"It's beautiful," I said with a sigh, even though my eyes only focused on the man before me and not the gorgeous home he'd procured, complete with a huge back yard for the dog we planned to adopt. Ryder's expression gave nothing away. When I was with him, he always seemed to hold sway on all the oxygen in my lungs, as if his mere presence could suck the very breath from my body.

"You're beautiful," he purred, that melodious voice, velvety as honey washing over me like a soothing rain after a humid day.

I met his soulful gaze, watching every nuance of his expression. I hadn't seen him like this since that night at Lutsen in our suite. So open and emotional. Ryder liked to keep himself stoic and staid, never allowing his love to precede his lust. But tonight, things were different. Because he'd proposed and I'd accepted. And now it was time to seal that promise with our bodies. I couldn't believe that just a few short hours ago, Ryder had surprised me with a five-carat diamond ring over dinner at Casa Fiorino. His planned proposal via tiramisu had quickly turned into a huge party, Eloise directing all the festivities from her usual place at the helm.

"What are you thinking about?" Ryder brought me back to the present as he nuzzled his face in my neck.

"That I love you," I whispered, wanting to drink in the joy on his face and lock it away inside my heart forever. "In this case, my first will be my last."

"And I love you, future Mrs. Martin. Can't say I'm upset about being your one and only."

Ryder was kind to me, but now there was more. I knew he adored me with every cell he possessed. That he'd keep me safe and protected. And cherished. Walter's death had changed him for the better. His walls had come tumbling down and he understood the importance of family. He even welcomed it. Just for me and our bright future. Even Eloise had to admit the change in the man by the right woman had been most profound.

I leaned into our embrace and cupped his cheeks, feeling the stubble there. I loved his sexy scruff. Loved scraping my soft face against his rough one. We were opposites in most ways. Soft and hard. Light and dark. But in this way, we fit like a glove as one. I captured his lips in a fierce kiss, and he reflected my passion right back to me with fervor of his own.

His arms came around me and he cupped the back of my head, angling me for easier access as he ravished my lips. I opened my mouth so he could taste me at his leisure. Ryder darted his tongue out, tracing the crease of my lips. When I gasped in pleasure, he took that opportunity to slide inside.

Ryder released me, and I slid down the length of his sinewy body. On the way down, I felt the swell of his cock sandwiched between us. My blood rushed through my veins, pulsing and throbbing. Every cell firing with pleasure. I looked up at him in the dim light, my eyes seeking everything he had to give.

"Ryder?" I said on a moan, my voice cracking under the depth of emotion I felt for him. My rock. My future husband. The father of my children. The man I wanted to grow old with as we sat on the front porch of this house. Or any house. Anywhere.

"Do you want to stop?" he asked and then smiled that charming grin that said he already knew the answer.

I knew he teased me, but I tugged on his sleeve just the same. "Never. Bedroom."

Ryder scooped me up, and in a few quick strides, I fell backward on the king-sized bed. He let his hand drift across my flat stomach and to my hip, tugging on the waistband of my pants. They came off in one motion and flew onto the carpet. Following the clothing to the ground, Ryder knelt between my legs. His soft palms caressed the inside of my thighs, stopping at the place I needed him most.

"This is all about you, Hannah," he said. "This night. This house. I want you to understand how deeply my feelings run.

There's only been you from the moment I saw your hair shining in the fluorescent lights of Casa Fiorino. I'm so glad I'm you're first and your last."

I nodded, unable to articulate anything that wouldn't spoil the perfection of the moment. I froze as Ryder's deft fingers opened the wet folds of my pussy and just settled his palm and allowed it to rest there when all I wanted was for his hand to move. To provide that delicious friction that I needed. I'd been craving it on the car ride over and had almost asked him to pull over and ease the ache.

His hot palm provided only a whisper of pressure. "I'm the only one to touch you here. To taste you. To slide my cock inside you. Your pretty pussy belongs to me. Do you know what that does to me, Hannah?"

"Please," I finally whimpered, allowing my eyes to flutter closed against the lusty look he gifted me as he continued the torment. "Please touch me, Ryder. It's always been you. Only you."

"Where?" he asked, still immobile. "Where do you want me to touch you, fiancée?"

God, all I wanted was for him to rip off his jeans and boxers, slide his cock inside me to the hilt and possess me. Claim me. Make me his for this moment and for every moment until the last star was counted.

But he hesitated. Watching. Waiting.

I tugged my lower lip between my teeth and slid my hand down to show him. "Touch my pussy, Ryder. Make me come. Please."

He rewarded my breathy admission by pressing his thumb against my throbbing clit, and I jolted, almost bucking off the edge of the bed. More like off the cliff of pleasure to soar downward toward a demise of pleasure. I started again when he slid one finger inside me, and I flexed around him, savoring the sensation.

"I love it when you say naughty words, sweet Hannah. It makes me so fucking hard. I have never seen anything more incredible than you. All sugar and spice." With his words, Ryder leaned over my body so he could use his free hand to remove my shirt. He pulled my lacy bra down to expose my erect nipples and captured one straining tip with his lips.

With a little mewl of pleasure, I relaxed into the sensations he created with his hands and mouth. Ryder moved his finger inside me as he swirled around my clit with his thumb and thrust in perfect time.

"No," I whimpered.

He looked up to meet my eyes. "What do you mean, no?"

I reached up to thread my fingers through his thick hair. "I don't want to come without your huge cock inside me. And I want it bare. I've wanted that since the first time... well, since that night."

"You don't have to ask me twice, my angel," he hissed. "I'm thirty now, it's time to think about a family. Right fucking now. Sorry, that you're marrying a geezer."

I chuckled, so happy to be myself and express all of my emotions in the bedroom and feel safe in doing so. Ryder Martin was a revelation. A pleasant surprise. And one hundred percent mine. As I watched in rapt fascination, he shrugged out of his clothes and threw them on the pile.

"Is this what you wanted?" He met my gaze as he gripped himself and pumped his steely dick a few times until a bead of moisture appeared at the tip.

I licked my lips and trailed my fingers up my inner thighs. "Yes."

Ryder loomed over me, caging me in with his massive body.

I felt the nudge of his cock at my slick entrance and waited for him to drive home. Like I wanted. Like I needed.

Snaking a hand around his trim waist, I yanked him toward me. "Now, Ryder. Release the swimmers."

"I'm pretty sure I have few little Michael Phelps wannabes down in my ball sac. I'm not dead yet," he said with that cocky grin as he kissed my lips.

Wanna-be. Hell, I'd never, ever be that version of Hannah again. Because Ryder made me the best version of myself, inspiring me to be the woman I'd become in his arms. I kissed him back with all the love I felt in my heart until the flow of emotion threatened to overwhelm me. Even saying his name seemed painful but it was a sinfully pleasurable ache. I wanted to whisper his name on the sigh of my moans like a benediction and taste it on my tongue even as he tasted my skin with his.

He leaned forward and thrust home. I shivered and moaned as I savored the blissful feeling of fullness. It seemed the ways this man made me happy were endless, and I looked forward to experiencing every single thing he would ever give me.

He slid out and then forward again, until he was buried balls deep. I shifted beneath him, and an electrifying jolt of pleasure pulsated on every nerve ending. I flexed my hips again until Ryder made an almost pained sound.

The strength of his groan ripped through him as he rolled my straining nipples between his fingers. "You're so tight and hot. God, I've never been inside a woman without a condom. I'm seeing stars here, Hannah."

Then Ryder began to move in earnest, slow at first but then grinding his cock in small circles as he possessed me with his entire body, knowing exactly how to get me off. The pleasure I'd felt from his fingers flashed back to life. I took huge handfuls of the bed sheets, writhing and lifting my molten hot core to meet his every motion and gasping for air as his speed increased.

The crest of pleasure came on a wave. I sensed its impending explosion and was helpless to numb the intensity. Didn't even want to. I wanted it to crash over me – to drown me in pleasure and surrender – and yet when it did, I didn't scream my release, I screamed Ryder's name along with a declaration of love that I'd never tire of saying.

His expression twisted in pleasure, his lips pressing together in a thin, white line and with a shout of ecstasy that echoed through my heart, he thrust one final time until I felt him come so deep inside me, the heat warmed my womb.

Ryder collapsed beside me and drew me to his torso in a warm embrace. I still couldn't believe life could be like this. That I could be this happy.

"That was amazing," he mumbled. "You're amazing. I love you so much, Hannah. I know I don't deserve you, but I'm going to thank God and my dad every single day that you're mine."

My heart pitched and soared, finding a soft landing right beside the man I loved. And even though his words had been said before, at that moment they rang fresh and new. Because they meant everything in the world.

ABOUT THE AUTHOR

"People are like stained-glass windows. They sparkle and shine when the sun is out, but when the darkness sets in, their true beauty is revealed only if there is a light from within."
— Elisabeth Kübler-Ross

Are you willing to discover the beauty within the flaws?

Then this is your tribe.

These are your books.

Colleen Charles is the USA Today Bestselling author of Perfectly Imperfect Romance for perfectly imperfect readers.

Take a chance and join her... you won't be sorry you did.

Colleen loves to hear from her readers and she answers all communications personally. You can find her at:

ColleenCharles.Com

Subscribe to my Newsletter online and receive email notices about new book releases, sales, and special promotions.

New subscribers receive an EXCLUSIVE FREE NOVEL as a special gift.

www.colleencharles.com/free

Made in the USA
Monee, IL
19 March 2022

93198854R00132